A Deadly Surprise

As Ned pushed the kayak into the water I felt something cold and slimy near my foot. Something cold, slimy—and moving!

"Omigod!" I cried, trying to jump up in the kayak. "Something's in here!"

Ned was standing waist-deep in the water as he shouted, "Nancy, don't stand up or you'll—"

"Whooaaa!" I cried as the kayak began to tip. I squeezed my eyes shut as I tumbled out of the boat and into the water.

"Nancy, are you all right?" Ned asked as he helped me out of the water.

"Look inside the cockpit, Ned," I said. "I know I felt something!"

Ned dragged the kayak out of the water and onto the bank. We peered into the cockpit, and I gasped. Curled inside was a *snake*!

NANCY DREW

Available from Aladdin

CAROLYN KEENE

NANCY DREW

GIRL DETECTIVE®

Stalk, Don't Run

#47

**Book Three in the
Malibu Mayhem Trilogy**

Aladdin
New York   London   Toronto   Sydney   New Delhi

❧ALADDIN
An imprint of Simon & Schuster Children's Publishing Division
1230 Avenue of the Americas, New York, NY 10020
First Aladdin paperback edition February 2012
Copyright © 2012 by Simon & Schuster, Inc.
All rights reserved, including the right of
reproduction in whole or in part in any form.
ALADDIN is a trademark of Simon & Schuster, Inc., and related logo is a registered trademark of Simon & Schuster, Inc.
NANCY DREW, NANCY DREW: GIRL DETECTIVE, and related logo are registered trademarks of Simon & Schuster, Inc.
For information about special discounts for bulk purchases, please contact Simon & Schuster Special Sales at 1-866-506-1949
or business@simonandschuster.com.
The Simon & Schuster Speakers Bureau can bring authors to your live event.
For more information or to book an event contact the Simon & Schuster Speakers Bureau at 1-866-248-3049 or visit our website at www.simonspeakers.com.
Designed by Karina Granda
The text of this book was set in Bembo.
Manufactured in the United States of America 0112 OFF
10 9 8 7 6 5 4 3 2 1
Library of Congress Control Number 2011934218
ISBN 978-1-4424-2299-5
ISBN 978-1-4424-2300-8 (eBook)

Contents

STRANGE HOUSE CALL

"**O**f all the people in River Heights, you're interviewing *us*?" I said, ripping a slice of pizza from the pie. "Must be a slow news week at the *Bugle*, Ned."

Ned Nickerson flashed one of his über-cute smiles. He'd been my boyfriend since junior high, but the way he looked at me with his brown eyes still made my heart do a triple flip.

When Ned wasn't dating me or studying English lit at our local university, he was honing his journalist chops at his dad's paper, the *River Heights Bugle*.

His latest assignment: interviewing me, Bess Marvin, and George Fayne about our latest case on trendy Malachite Beach in Malibu, California. As the four of us sat in Sylvio's Pizzeria sharing a jumbo mushroom and olive pie I couldn't think of a better—or yummier—place to do business.

"Think about it," Ned said, passing the oregano to George. "You just got back from three weeks in California, where you blew the whistle on a crazy cult leader, apprehended a fugitive, and cracked the case of a mysterious oil spill. This story is going to be huge!"

"Did we do all that?" George teased. She held her slice up and let the oil drip into her mouth.

Bess shot George a disgusted look as she neatly cut her slice with a knife and fork. She and George were as different as pepperoni and anchovies, which made it hard for anyone, including me, to believe they were actually first cousins.

"Do people still read newspapers?" George asked. "I usually get my news online."

"You'd get *air* online if it were possible, George," Bess joked.

"The *Bugle* has a huge readership," Ned said. "Not just in River Heights, but in surrounding cities and towns."

"Cool," Bess said excitedly. "Will our article be

on the same page as the fashion news or the horo-scopes?"

"Are you kidding?" Ned asked. "Try page four."

Bess gasped and said, "That's the River Heights Spotlight—the most-read section of the paper."

"Besides the sports page," George said. "Okay, I admit to picking up a newspaper every once in a while."

"Page four will be awesome, Ned," I said with a smile. "Thanks."

Ned smiled back with a little wink. He was smart and handsome and nice—no wonder so many girls in River Heights had crushes on him. Luckily, the only one I had to worry about was Deirdre Shannon. Deirdre was the daughter of a super-successful attor-ney, and whatever she wanted, she got. That was okay with me, as long as she didn't get Ned.

"Nancy?" Ned interrupted my thoughts. "I have another question. It's about Roland."

Roland. Ugh. The mere mention of the crazy cult leader's name made my skin crawl. "What about him?" I asked with a frown.

"Was he really that evil?" Ned asked, pushing a digital recorder closer to me. "I mean, did he really abuse his followers?"

"Depends on how you define abuse," I said. "Roland used mind games to get his followers to walk across hot coals and sit for hours in an airless sweat lodge."

"He and his sidekick Inge injected those poor people with a mind-altering drug they thought was vitamins," Bess said.

Ned whistled through his teeth. "I'd call that abuse," he said. "What did the oil spill have to do with Roland?"

"We thought Roland had blown himself up in his yacht to keep the police from taking him alive," I explained. "The explosion caused an oil spill that damaged Malachite Beach and its wildlife."

"Turns out it wasn't Roland who blew up the yacht," George said. "It was our gracious hostess, Stacey Manning."

George said the word "gracious" with a sprinkle of sarcasm. Stacey, a star Hollywood party planner, had lent us her trendy Malachite Beach house for three whole weeks. Little did we know she and Roland had planned something a lot more sinister than a party.

"If Stacey blew up Roland's yacht," Ned said slowly, "then . . . what happened to Roland?"

"Bess, George, and I discovered that Roland had plastic surgery to totally alter his appearance," I said.

"Now he's on the run," Bess said with a sigh.

"You mean the crazy cult leader who almost

killed dozens of people is still out there?" Ned said. "Did the police ever question the plastic surgeon? He must have been in on it."

"You mean the world-famous Dr. Raymond?" George snorted. "Yeah, the police questioned him."

"Dr. Raymond insisted he didn't know Roland's sinister intentions," Bess said. "He even described to the police what Roland would look like now."

"So, what does he look like?" Ned asked.

"According to Dr. Raymond, Roland has a receding hairline, a cleft chin, and a long, angular nose," I said.

"I'll bet Roland dyed his hair from blond to dark," Bess said. She tossed her long blond hair and added, "That must have been the hardest part."

"Give me a break," George said, popping a mushroom into her mouth.

Ned studied the three of us. "Maybe I'm wrong, but you don't seem worried that Roland is somewhere out there," he said.

I shrugged. "That's because Dr. Raymond gave the police a concise description of Roland. Hopefully the psycho is being picked up as we speak."

We took a short break from Ned's interview as Sylvio brought us some of his famous garlic knots.

"Thanks, Sylvio," Ned said. "Add it to my bill."

"Bill, schmill!" Sylvio said, wiping his hands on his apron. "It's on the house!"

"Really?" I asked.

"Sure!" Sylvio boomed. He pressed his hand to his heart. "It is an honor to have River Heights's own girl detectives in my humble establishment. I might even name a pie after you girls someday!"

"Sweet!" Bess said with a giggle. "As long as it doesn't have anchovies."

"I guess we are celebrities in this town," George said as Sylvio hurried back to the counter.

"Speaking of celebrities," Ned said. "I hope you don't mind my next question."

"Ask away," I said.

"Okay," Ned said, leaning over with a gleam in his eye. "What were the Casabian sisters really like?"

What? Had Ned Nickerson, rising star reporter, just asked me about the Casabian sisters?

"You mean Mandy, Mallory, and Mia?" I said. "Don't tell me you watch their ditzy reality show too, Ned."

"Um . . . I might have seen it once," he said, blushing a bit. "Or . . . twice."

"Oh, Ned." I groaned.

"Hey, give me a break," Ned said. "I'm only asking because you rescued the youngest sister from Roland's cult. You did, didn't you?"

"We sure did," Bess said. "Nancy and I pretended to be followers of Roland so we could infiltrate his cult and save Mia."

"Wait a minute, Ned," George said. "I thought the *River Heights Bugle* was a serious paper and that your dad refuses to print celebrity gossip. So what's up?"

"We don't print celebrity gossip," Ned said. "My question about the sisters was a personal one—and totally off the record."

"Yeah, well, those annoying sisters and their dumb show are back on Malachite Beach where they belong," George said. "I hope we never see those three again."

"Whoa!" Bess said. She nodded at the recorder. "Make sure that's off the record too, Ned."

"No problem," Ned said as he turned off his tape recorder. "In fact . . . my interview is over."

We finished our pizza and plowed into Sylvio's complimentary garlic knots. Being with Ned and my friends at our favorite hangout reminded me how happy I was to be back home in River Heights.

Sure, Malachite Beach was exclusive and beautiful—especially before the oil spill. But the little midwestern city of River Heights would always be home.

"Guess what, Nancy?" Ned said as he slipped

his recorder into his canvas messenger bag. "I just bought my friend Dave's old kayak. It seats two, so we can go paddling on the river together."

"Great," I said. "But we'll have to do that when I'm not working my summer job, Ned."

"You just got back. Already working on a new case?" Ned asked.

"Not exactly a case," I said. "Yesterday I landed a part-time job at Safer's Cheese Shop on Main Street."

"Safer's?" Ned asked, surprised. "Not very intriguing for a rising detective superstar."

"Which is exactly why I asked Mr. Safer if he needed help," I said. "I wanted to do something totally down-to-earth and predictable for a change. At least for the rest of the summer."

"After what we went through in Malachite and with Roland," George said, "boring is the new black!"

But working at Safer's would be anything but boring. Mr. Safer was a Broadway theater fanatic. He was known throughout River Heights for singing show tunes behind the counter—and even making his customers join in on the chorus.

After we left Sylvio's, Ned kissed me good-bye and headed for the *Bugle* office. As I walked down Main Street with Bess and George, they shared their own plans for the summer—or at least what was left of it.

"I'm helping my dad arrange his toolshed," Bess said. "It was just painted, so all the tools and equipment have to be returned to their correct places."

"Sounds riveting," George joked.

"It is for Bess," I said with a smile.

Bess might be totally girly, with her perfectly blown-out blond hair and cutting-edge outfits, but in a flash she could roll up her sleeves and build or fix anything. George could fix anything too—as long as it was high-tech or electronic. That's why she would be spending the summer fixing and upgrading computers, MP3 players, even mobile phones.

"It's time you got a new phone, Nancy," George said, nodding at the one in my hand. "It's practically retro."

"I thought retro was cool," I said.

Bess saw me reading a new text and said, "Let me guess. It's from Ned. He misses you already and can't live without you. Right?"

"Wrong. It's Hannah," I said with a grin. "She wants me to pick up olive oil and a container of ricotta cheese."

"It's just an errand," George said. "So . . . why do you look so excited?"

"It's a clue that Hannah is making her amazing

baked ziti," I said. "She must have really missed me. Ever since I got home she's been baking and cooking all my favorite foods—day and night."

Hannah Gruen was much more than a housekeeper. For years she had been just like a mother to me. Sure, I missed my real mom, who died when I was only three—but Hannah was truly part of my family.

I was about to pocket my phone when a new text came in. This one wasn't from Hannah or Ned. In fact, I couldn't identify the sender by its number or name.

"It's from somebody called 'Shanager,'" I said. I read the message out loud. "'N,B,G—go to 1717 Water Street ASAP.'"

"Who's Shanager?" Bess asked.

I shrugged and said, "I have no idea."

"Isn't 1717 the old house with the peeling paint that's been empty for more than a year?" George asked.

"Didn't someone die in it?" Bess asked uneasily.

"I think so," I said. "I guess I should text back, huh?"

"You should ignore it, that's what you should do, Nancy," George said. "Sounds like a prank, if you ask me."

"Yeah, Nance," Bess said. "For all we know, this

Shanager is a dangerous kook—or another crazy cult leader like Roland—"

"Bess," I cut in. "We're not on Malachite Beach anymore—we're home in River Heights. What can go wrong here?"

"A lot," Georges admitted. "Or we wouldn't be in business."

I stared at my phone, more intrigued than worried. Who was this Shanager? Why did he or she want us to go to the house?

"I want to check it out," I said.

"There you go following another clue, Nancy," Bess said. "Whatever happened to wanting a nice, boring summer?"

"I've been solving mysteries since I was eight years old, Bess," I said. "Don't stop me now."

Bess needed a little more convincing, but after I suggested that it might be a "Welcome Back to River Heights" surprise party, she caved.

The three of us set out for Water Street, finding the house at the end of the block. Instead of looking broken-down and abandoned, it had a fresh coat of paint, new windows, and a neatly mowed lawn.

"That's funny," I said as we made our way up the flagstone path through the front yard. "I didn't know it was renovated."

"Which makes it even weirder," Bess said.

The wooden porch, also painted, creaked as we stepped on it. There was a brass knocker on the front door, but I chose to ring the shiny new doorbell. We'd waited a mere ten seconds when Bess blurted, "No surprise party here. Time to go."

"See?" George said. "I warned you."

"Wait!" I said as another text came through. "It's that Shanager again."

"What does this one say?" Bess asked.

"'See you in the back,'" I read out loud.

This time I quickly texted back, WHY?

The reply: YOU'LL SEE.

"Just ignore it, Nancy," George said firmly. "Let's go."

"No way." I waved my friends off the porch. "Let's see if this Shanager is waiting in the back."

"With a chain saw," Bess said.

The three of us rounded the house to the backyard. No one was there. Almost immediately my phone went off with another text.

"Shanager again?" George asked.

"We're being watched," Bess said quietly.

I read the text. "Shanager wants us to proceed to the cellar door and open at our own risk."

The sensible, mature part of me said, *Don't even think about it*. The curious detective part told me, *Go for it*.

"Nancy Drew," George cried as I made a beeline for the cellar door. "Are you nuts?"

Before my friends could talk me out of it, I grabbed the handle on the door and pulled it open.

Looking down into the cellar, I saw only darkness. I'd taken one step when I felt a bony hand grab my ankle.

Needle-sharp nails dug into my flesh. The coldest chill ran up my spine. I screamed, "Bess, George! HELP!"

REALITY CHECK

I could hear Bess scream as I tried to loosen the grip. What had I been thinking, opening the stupid door? Shanager *was* probably a serial killer!

From the corner of my eye I saw George grab a nearby shovel. She was about to bring it down on the hand when—

"Stop! I let go, okay?" a voice shouted from below. It was a female voice, definitely familiar. When she climbed out of the basement, I could see why. . . .

"Mallory?" I cried as the middle Casabian sister

brushed herself off. A few seconds later her two sisters climbed out behind her.

"Mandy? Mia?" Bess said incredulously.

"So one of you was Shanager?" George asked.

The sisters didn't answer George's question. Instead Mallory wiggled her fingers and said, "Sorry if I scratched your ankle, Nancy. I didn't mean to hold on so tightly."

"It's about time you guys got here," Mandy told us. "That cellar was grossing me out!"

"It was really dark, too," Mia said. She blinked to adjust her eyes to the light before slipping on a pair of cool tortoiseshell shades.

I couldn't care less about the gross cellar. All I wanted to know was—

"What are you doing in River Heights?" I asked.

"Let me guess," George said with a frown. "You meant to enter Rodeo Drive on your GPS and goofed."

"So not!" Mandy said, shaking her head. "We happen to be in River Heights for a good reason."

Mallory swept her hand toward the house. "Welcome to Casa Bonita!" she declared. "That means 'beautiful house' in Spanish."

"I like to think it means beautiful houseguests," Mandy said, flipping her long, dark hair over her shoulder.

"Houseguests?" Bess asked. "You mean you live here?"

"Just temporarily," Mandy explained. "We're here to try out a concept for a new reality show we're planning to pitch."

Oh, help. It seemed like everybody—including the Casabian sisters—had a reality show in Los Angeles, but what did that have to do with River Heights?

"The show would be called *Get Real with the Casabians*," Mia said. "The idea is we would live in a real house in a real town just like here."

"Instead of making appearances at movie premieres, clubs, and Hollywood parties," Mandy continued, "we'd try out *real* jobs in *real* places."

"Like banks, grocery stores," Mallory added. "Hopefully beauty salons and spas—if there are any here."

I still didn't get it. Mandy, Mallory, and Mia already *had* a reality show called *Chillin' with the Casabians*. Their producer and camera crew on Malachite Beach followed them everywhere they went.

"So . . . you'd have two reality shows?" I asked.

"Omigod—no!" Mia said with a shudder. "The other show was canceled. The network said the episodes became too disturbing. You know, with the cult and the sweat lodge and all."

Mia's face fell while she spoke about the cult and the sweat lodge. Out of all the sisters, she was the most sensible one, but also the most vulnerable. She had fallen under Roland's spell, joining his cult and becoming totally brainwashed.

Thanks to us, Mia had been rescued from the cult, but she obviously still harbored awful memories of it.

"Of course it got too disturbing," George told the sisters. "Your camera crew followed you wherever you went."

She looked around before saying, "Where's your crew hiding now? And that pushy producer of yours . . . what was her name . . . Beth?"

"It was Bev, but don't worry," Mandy said. "There'll be no cameras until the show gets picked up."

"This is so awesome," Bess said excitedly. "With all the towns in the United States, what made you pick River Heights?"

"Yeah," George said, not as excited. "What makes us so special?"

"While you were staying on Malachite Beach, you told us about your hometown," Mandy said. "When we decided to stay in a small town, we thought of River Heights."

"She means *quaint*," Mia said quickly.

"Hold on, you guys," I said. "River Heights is anything but quaint. We have a university, thriving businesses—"

"A modern shopping complex, parks," Bess put in. "There's even the River Heights Theater with its own company."

"Okay, okay!" Mandy said. "We get it."

"The most important thing is that we wanted to go somewhere where we've never, ever been to before," Mallory said.

The Casabian sisters invited us inside. Once there I saw brand-new furniture and freshly painted walls.

"It's not exactly Villa Fabuloso," Mandy said. "But it'll do, even if we have to lift open the garage door all by ourselves."

It certainly wasn't Villa Fabuloso—the sisters' private villa on Malachite Beach in Malibu—but how many homes were?

I looked at the sisters' suitcases and duffel bags, still unpacked in the entrance hall.

"Who are you here with?" I asked. "Your agent . . . your manager?"

The sisters traded grins.

"That was our next surprise," Mandy told us. "Since our manager dropped us after the show was canceled, we hired a temporary manager right here in River Heights. She's upstairs. Let me call her."

But before Mandy could say a word, a pair of black high heels came down the staircase, followed by someone I knew well. *Too* well.

"Deirdre Shannon." I groaned under my breath.

Deirdre stopped at the bottom of the stairs. In her black suit, she looked more like the CEO of a company than an eighteen-year-old. "Nancy, Bess, George," she said coolly. "I see you've met my clients."

Clients? The Casabian sisters' new manager was Deirdre Shannon?

"So you were Shanager," Bess told Deirdre.

Deirdre nodded and said, "Shannon . . . manager. You mean you didn't figure it out, girl detectives?"

Bess, George, and I were too stunned to say another word. As Deirdre breezed past us to the sisters, she said, "I'm not officially their manager . . . yet. For now, I'm going to help Mandy, Mallory, and Mia land jobs here in River Heights."

"When the show gets picked up," Mandy said, "we'll work out a more permanent situation."

"How did you find Deirdre?" I asked the sisters.

"We found Mr. Shannon first," Mandy said. "We called him, thinking he was a real estate agent who could help us locate a furnished rental house."

"We had no idea he was a lawyer," Mia said. "He put us in touch with a real estate agent and with Deirdre."

George looked at Deirdre. "So, Daddy got you your new job?" she said.

"So what?" Deirdre said. "With all my connections in this town I'm just what Mandy, Mallory, and Mia need. Besides . . . River Heights could use some real celebrities for a change." She laughed.

I had an idea that was for our benefit, but I wasn't letting Deirdre off so easy.

"If you're such a good manager, Dee-Dee," I said, using Deirdre's hated nickname, "why didn't anyone know that the sisters were in town?"

"Yeah," Bess said. "Didn't you alert the media?"

"What media?" Mandy asked. "The only paper around here is some free one called the *River Heights Trumpet*."

"You mean the *River Heights Bugle*, Mandy," I said. "And it's anything but a PennySaver."

"We just did an interview for the *Bugle*," Bess said proudly. "It'll be in tomorrow's edition. Page four!"

Deirdre tapped her chin thoughtfully, which told me her conniving wheels were spinning. "Which reminds me," she said. "I have to contact Ned Nickerson. Maybe he can write a story in the *Bugle* about the sisters being in town."

Hearing Deirdre mention Ned made me want to shriek. There she went again, trying to get near my boyfriend, but I forced a smile and through gritted teeth said, "Good luck."

Mandy, Mallory, and Mia saw us to the front door.

We waved good-bye to them as we walked away from the house. Once we were out of earshot, I said, "Good luck is right. Deirdre will never get Ned to write an article about the Casabians for the *Bugle*."

"You're right about that," Bess said. "The *Bugle* doesn't do celebrity gossip. Period."

"I still can't believe Mandy, Mallory, and Mia are in River Heights," George said, shaking her head. "They better not try to turn this place into Malachite Beach!"

"We can only hope!" Bess said, her eyes lighting up. "Deirdre was right when she said we never had such famous celebrities around."

"That may be true," I said as we walked up Water Street. "But *we're* going to be on page four of the *Bugle* tomorrow."

The three of us traded high fives.

"I have an idea," Bess said. "Why don't we meet tomorrow morning at my house when the paper arrives? That way we can all read it together."

"We'd have to wake up at the crack of dawn," George said with a groan.

"Works for me," I said. "Since Hannah is on a baking and cooking roll, I'll ask her to whip up some of her famous cinnamon buns."

George grinned and said, "Now *that's* worth waking up for."

As we turned the corner I said, "Isn't it great to be home and back to normal again?"

"With the Casabian sisters in town?" George said. "Trust me—nothing will ever be normal again."

For the rest of the day I couldn't stop thinking about Mandy, Mallory, and Mia—and Deirdre. Her new job as their manager seemed to prove that she really did get whatever she wanted.

But I have something she wants but can't get, I reminded myself. *Ned Nickerson.*

That night I turned my thoughts from the Casabians to someone sinister: Roland!

While my dad watched two lawyers arguing on TV, I browsed the web for any information I could get about the runaway cult leader.

All I could find besides old articles about Roland's disappearance was the website for his notorious and defunct Renewal Retreat and Spa. The sight of his logo made me gulp—a bright yellow sunburst with shimmering rays.

How could a psycho madman like Roland come up with such a cheery design? I wondered.

During the commercial Dad turned to me from his favorite spot on the sofa. "What are you so busy with tonight?" he asked with a smile. "You couldn't possibly be working on a case, could you?"

"Well, yes," I said. "It's about one particular enemy on the lam."

"You mean Roland?" Dad said with a frown.

"Exactly," I said. "So far there's nothing about Roland being arrested—which means he's still somewhere out there."

Dad gave me his serious lawyerly look—the one he used when helping me with my cases.

"You've got to be patient, Nancy, and trust that Roland will be apprehended sooner or later," he said.

"But he had plastic surgery, Dad," I said. "Major plastic surgery to look like a totally different person."

"You can change your appearance," Dad said. "But you can never disguise evil."

Wow. Dad never ceased to surprise me. He was right.

"Smoothie break!" Hannah's voice called out.

I turned to see her carrying two tall smoothie glasses into the den.

"Hannah, I'm going to gain ten pounds!" I said, smiling as I took the glass. "And it will definitely be worth it!"

Later I had no trouble falling asleep. But some-time in the middle of the night my deep sleep was interrupted by a sudden jangling tune. At first I thought it was part of my dream—until I realized it was the ring tone of my phone.

Who was calling me in the middle of the night? Who was calling me at all? My friends usually texted. My first thought was the Casabian sisters. They were probably still on California time.

I fumbled in the dark for my phone and pulled it to my ear. "Hello?" I said groggily.

No answer.

"Hello?" I asked again. "Who's there?"

By now I was wide awake, sitting up in bed. I listened for any sign of life on the other end. Was it just dead air? Then I heard a faint click.

I turned to the menu, checking the last incoming call. It was labeled UNKNOWN.

"Great," I told myself.

There was something creepy about getting a strange call in the middle of the night—especially when the person on the other end didn't say a word.

I tried telling myself it was a wrong number as I turned off my phone. What else could it be?

You're not on Malachite Beach anymore, Nancy. Relax, I thought as I fell back on my pillow.

• • •

"Do you have the cinnamon buns, Nancy?" Hannah called from the doorstep while I made my way to the car.

"Got them," I called back, lifting the plastic container in my hands. "Thanks again, Hannah."

She gave me a thumbs-up before going into the house.

I drove toward the Marvin house, surrounded by the smell of warm cinnamon and vanilla. It was then that I decided to deliver some cinnamon buns to my new—if only temporary—neighbors, Mandy, Mallory, and Mia.

I steered my trusty hybrid onto Water Street, parked at the curb, and carried the container up the flagstone path to the front door.

"Casa Bonita," I said to myself. Leave it to the Casabians to make an ordinary house in River Heights sound like a villa on Malachite Beach.

I rang the doorbell and waited. I knew it was early, especially for the sisters, but as George said, Hannah's cinnamon buns were worth waking up for at any hour.

After ringing several times—with no answer—I figured the Casabians probably had jet lag.

"So much for that idea," I decided.

I was about to leave when I heard thumping noises from inside the house, followed by one loud *thud*.

What was that? I wondered.

Placing the container on the porch, I raced to a window and peered inside the house.

Sprawled at the bottom of the stairs was Mandy!

CARELESS OR RUTHLESS

banged on the window and called Mandy's name over and over. She didn't move a muscle.

Desperate to get inside, I tried opening the front windows, but no luck.

The garage! I thought, jumping off the porch.

I remembered Mandy saying it had one of those old-fashioned garage doors—the kind you lifted up and down. When I pulled the door up, I heard the sound of a car engine . . . running!

Carbon monoxide! I thought in a panic. Carbon monoxide was colorless, odorless, and deadly!

"How could they leave the car on?" I asked

myself as I ran toward the car. "How can they be so stupid?"

I flung the car door open, found the keys, and turned off the engine. Then I bolted through the side door into the house.

Was I too late? Had the noxious gas killed the Casabian sisters?

The windows were easier to open from inside. As fresh air blew into the house, I ran to Mandy and touched her neck. Her pulse was throbbing. She was still alive.

"Mandy, sit up," I said, lightly slapping her face.

Mandy mumbled something I couldn't understand. But I had to leave her at the staircase to check on Mallory and Mia.

Thundering upstairs, I found the sisters in the same bedroom. After opening every window in the room, I took turns shaking Mallory and Mia.

"Wake up!" I called over and over.

Mia's eyes fluttered open. "My head is killing me," she said in a raspy voice.

"Mine too," Mallory mumbled.

After helping them sit up, I said, "Headaches are one of the symptoms of carbon monoxide poisoning. The other is death."

"Carbon monoxide?" Mia asked. "But how—"

"I don't know. Are there any carbon monoxide alarms in the house?" I asked. "Your car was running—you forgot to turn it off."

"Nuh-uh!" Mandy's voice said.

Turning, I saw Mandy leaning against the door frame. She still looked pale and groggy but had managed to walk up the stairs. A good sign.

"What do you mean, nuh-uh?" I asked.

"I remember turning the car off after I parked it in the garage," Mandy said.

"I saw her do it," Mallory said. "It's a rental car, so she was trying to figure out how it worked."

"Then why were the keys left in the car too?" I asked.

"Oops," Mandy said with a shrug. "That was me."

I cocked my head as I studied the sisters. As spaced-out as they were from the CO, they did seem pretty adamant about turning off the engine.

"So if you guys didn't leave the engine running, who did?" I asked.

"Nancy, what are you saying? " Mallory said, her eyes wide. "Do you think somebody sneaked into our garage to turn on our car?"

"Most of River Heights doesn't even know we're here yet," Mandy said.

I thought about it. The idea of someone killing the Casabian sisters—especially in River Heights—was kind of wild.

"Come on," I said, nodding toward the door. "I'll drive you to the emergency room so they can check you out."

"The hospital?" Mandy shook her head. "Not an option."

"Deirdre doesn't want us to go public yet," Mallory said, swinging her legs over the bed. "Anyway, I feel much, much better now."

"Me too," Mia said. "In fact, I could use some coffee and a little breakfast."

I remembered the plastic container I'd left out on the porch. "In that case," I said with a smile, "cinnamon buns, anyone?"

The Casabians and I ate Hannah's sweet specialty. Soon it was past eight, and I had to get to the Marvins' before the *Bugle* arrived.

As I drove, I couldn't stop thinking about the close carbon monoxide call. *Could* someone have broken into the sisters' garage to turn on the car and poison them? They were celebrities—and with celebrities came stalkers and wackos.

Once at the Marvin house, I raised the question with Bess and George.

"It does seem kind of weird," Bess said, licking frosting off her fingers.

"Especially since no one knows the sisters are here yet," George said.

"Hey, speaking of weird," I said, remembering something else that happened. "I got a call in the middle of the night."

"Who was it?" George asked.

"There was no one at the other end," I said.

George groaned under her breath. "Quit it, Nancy," she said. "Will you please just quit it?"

"Quit what?" I asked.

"Quit thinking too much," George said. "The call you got probably was a wrong number, and the sisters are such flakes it's no surprise they left the car running."

I didn't bother telling George that Mandy, Mallory, and Mia insisted they'd turned off the car. She probably wouldn't believe it anyway.

"Whatever," I said. "Fortunately, I got there in time to wake them up."

"And speaking of sisters, here comes mine," Bess said with a little sigh.

I looked up to see Bess's twelve-year-old sister, Maggie, race into the kitchen. She was wearing leggings and an Austin Gruber T-shirt.

Austin was the famous teenage singer who Bess, George, and I met while solving our case in Malachite. For a while Austin was a suspect, but after we cleared him of sabotaging Stacey Manning's fund-raising party, he became our friend.

"Cinnamon buns! Bring it!" Maggie squealed. She leaned over the table to grab a bun when—

"Step away from the cinnamon buns!" Mrs. Marvin's voice snapped. "I repeat, Maggie, step away from the buns!"

Maggie's hand froze over the plate. "Mom! You know I can eat a gazillion of these."

"Which is exactly why you're going to Camp Athena," Mrs. Marvin said, folding her arms. "And not a moment too soon."

"You're going to camp this summer, Maggie?" I asked.

Maggie nodded, but not happily.

"I've never heard of Camp Athena," George said.

"That's because it's a *boot* camp!" Maggie said with a scowl. "It's not fair. You guys got to hang with Austin Gruber this summer, and I get shipped off to do hard labor."

"Hey, we brought you back an Austin Gruber T-shirt," George told Maggie.

I couldn't get past the words Maggie had used to describe Camp Athena.

"Excuse me, Mrs. Marvin," I said. "Why is Maggie going to a boot camp?"

"Camp Athena is anything but boot camp," Mrs. Marvin said. "Maggie eats way too much junk food when she's around her friends, which is why I looked into Camp Athena in the first place."

Maggie rolled her eyes.

"Camp Athena is a camp that encourages healthy lifestyles, including positive thinking, exercise, and healthy eating," Mrs. Marvin explained. "And it's right here in River Heights."

"Wait a minute. I think I saw something about that camp online," George said. "Isn't it run by a woman named Amy?"

"Yes!" Mrs. Marvin said with a smile. "Amy Paloma is a rising star in girls' health. In fact, she was a guest last week on *Rise and Shine, River Heights*."

"Going to camp is neat, Maggie," I said, trying to cheer her up. "You'll play sports, do arts and crafts, make s'mores—"

"S'mores—as if," Maggie snorted. "We'll probably eat birdseed and rabbit food."

"I've already checked out the camp and was very impressed," Mrs. Marvin told us. "I'm taking Maggie there today to see for herself."

"Can't I go with Bess instead?" Maggie asked.

"Me?" Bess asked.

Maggie nodded and said, "If you like it, I'll go. If you don't, I won't."

"Oh, Maggie." Mrs. Marvin sighed. She turned to Bess and said, "Will you go with her?"

"I was going to start working on Dad's shed today, Mom," Bess said.

"*Please*, Bess?" Maggie begged. "It'll only take a few minutes to check out that stupid camp."

I wanted so badly to eat another cinnamon bun, but I didn't want to tempt Maggie. I was also curious about Camp Athena and Amy Paloma. Was she really so dynamic?

"I'll go too, Bess," I said.

"So will I," George said. "If they have computers, maybe I can drum up some business."

"Okay, okay," Bess said. "We'll all go to Camp Athena later this morning."

"Yes!" Maggie said. She turned to her mom. "Now can I have a cinnamon bun? If I go to Camp Athena, I may never see food again."

Mrs. Marvin chuckled, then said, "You can have half of one."

I tore a bun in half and shared it with Maggie. Just as I was about to pop it in my mouth, we heard a *thunk!*

"The *Bugle*'s here!" Bess said, jumping up from her chair.

The three of us raced outside, where the *River*

Heights Bugle lay on the doorstep. Bess turned to page four and sang, "Ta-daaaa!"

George and I peered over her shoulder at the page. Splashed across the River Heights Spotlight section wasn't an article about us, but a photo of Mandy, Mallory, and Mia!

"'River Heights Welcomes the Casabians,'" Bess read the headline. "'By Ned Nickerson.'"

"Ned?" I gasped. "This page four article is supposed to be about *us*."

"I thought the *River Heights Bugle* didn't print cheesy celebrity gossip," George said angrily.

"They do now," Bess said. "I wonder what changed their minds."

"What—or *who*," I said, narrowing my eyes. "Deirdre said she wanted to talk to Ned about running a piece on the Casabians."

"Whatever Deirdre Shannon wants," Bess said with a sigh, "Deirdre gets." She closed the paper as we sulked back into the house.

"I guess Deirdre was right in one way," I said.

"What?" George asked.

"Mandy, Mallory, and Mia are bigger celebrities than we are," I said. "Especially here in River Heights."

We swallowed our disappointment and the rest of Hannah's cinnamon buns.

• • •

A couple of hours later, the four of us piled into Bess's car for the drive to Camp Athena.

Once we arrived, Bess parked the car outside the camp gate. I was impressed by the two topiaries flanking the gate, trimmed to resemble Greek goddesses.

We filed through the gate and gazed at the campgrounds. There were several wooden bunks and a few larger cabins I guessed were the arts and crafts cabin, the theater, and the mess hall. Maggie seemed interested in checking out the other campers. Some girls, who looked about ten years old, were following their counselor to the tennis court. Another group of girls, dressed in bathing suits, were heading for what looked like a pool on a hill.

"Look," Bess said. "That's probably Amy Paloma."

I followed Bess's gaze to see a tanned woman with honey-blond hair walking over to us. She wore khaki shorts and a crisp white camp T-shirt. A shiny silver whistle hung around her neck.

"Welcome to Camp Athena," the woman greeted us. "I'm Amy Paloma."

She extended her hand to Maggie and said, "I'll bet you're Maggie Marvin. Your mom called to say you were visiting today."

"Hello," Maggie said, politely shaking Amy's hand.

"I'm Maggie's sister, Bess," Bess introduced herself. "And these are my friends Nancy and George."

"George?" Amy said, grinning at George. "How I love names that are not gender specific. How progressive of your parents to give you such a strong name as George."

"Her real name is Georgia," Maggie said.

George squirmed, as she always did whenever someone used her given name.

"Can we have a tour of the camp?" I asked, trying to change the subject.

"Yes, of course," Amy said. "Follow me."

The four of us walked with Amy as she proudly showed us around Camp Athena.

"Our bunks are named after Greek goddesses such as Demeter, Artemis, and Diana," Amy explained.

"What about Aphrodite?" Bess asked.

Amy shook her head. "It's not that I have anything against the goddess of beauty, but here at Camp Athena we strive first for wisdom and empowerment."

After showing us the pool and the volleyball and tennis courts, Amy took us to the dining hall. She explained that she hated the term "mess hall"— "Too negative," she said.

Some campers and counselors were eating an early lunch, chatting as they passed bowls and juice bottles.

"What are they eating?" Maggie asked.

"Veggie burgers and sweet potato fries," Amy said. "For dessert we have a melon salad with crushed walnuts."

"Sounds decent," Maggie said sincerely.

The campers seemed friendly and happy to be at Camp Athena. Three girls were even wearing Casabian Sisters T-shirts.

"I see you have some fans of Mandy, Mallory, and Mia," I told Amy.

Amy bristled, then spoke. "I try not to encourage celebrity worship here—especially of those sisters—but it's also important for the girls to express their interests."

"Look over there," Bess said, pointing to one of the tables. "Don't we know that girl?"

I looked to see where Bess was pointing. Sitting at the end of the table was a camper I recognized right away.

"That's Alice Bothwell!" I said with a smile.

"You mean the future mayor of Malachite Beach?" George said, smiling too. "No way!"

"You know Alice?" Amy asked.

"We met her while we were in California," I said.

"Alice helped us with a huge save-the-beach party back at Malachite. It was her idea."

"That sounds like Alice," Amy said. "She definitely has a can-do attitude."

By now Alice had spotted us, too. Amy motioned to her to come over, and she did, all smiles.

"I *thought* you guys lived in River Heights!" Alice said excitedly.

"What are you doing here, Alice?" I asked. "When we left Malachite, you were still busy cleaning up the beach."

"My mom wanted me to take a break," Alice said with a shrug. "She thought Camp Athena would be perfect for me."

"Is it?" Amy asked.

"For sure!" Alice confirmed. "Even if it is thousands of miles from Malachite Beach."

"You're not the only one here from Malachite Beach," Bess said. "The Casabian—"

George quickly clamped her hand over Bess's mouth.

"Never mind," Bess murmured through the hand.

I glanced at Maggie, who seemed to be examining what the campers were eating.

"The food here does look pretty good," Maggie said. "I thought they'd be serving rabbit food."

"So not!" Alice said with a chuckle. "We save the rabbit food for our rabbits."

"You have rabbits here?" Maggie asked.

"Three of them," Alice said. She looked up at Amy. "Mind if I show Maggie the camp zoo? I already finished lunch."

"You have a zoo here too?" I asked, surprised.

"Well, a nature center," Amy said. "I want all campers to appreciate different species."

Alice accompanied us on our trek to see the animals. I could see her pointing out camp sights to Maggie as they walked a few feet ahead.

"FYI," I whispered to Bess. "Looks like Maggie made a new friend."

"*If* she decides to come here," Bess whispered back. "Fingers crossed."

When we reached a small hut, we found guinea pigs, rabbits—even a snake coiled up in a Plexiglas tank.

"Whoa!" George said as we gazed at the olive-colored snake with the black bandit mask.

"Don't worry," Amy said. "The tank has a solid and very secure lid. The small openings are for ventilation."

"Sometimes I help the nature counselor feed the animals and clean the tanks and pens," Alice said.

"Why am I not surprised?" I asked.

Maggie was still staring at the snake, her eyes wide. "Is that a rattlesnake?" she asked.

"Slithers is a Florida cottonmouth," Amy explained. "They're totally rare here in the Midwest, so I had her imported from the South."

"Cool!" Maggie said. "Amy, once I'm a camper, can I visit the zoo whenever I like?"

"As long as it's on your bunk's schedule," Amy said.

"Is there room for me in Alice's bunk?" Maggie asked.

"We have two bunks for twelve-year-olds, Bunk Diana and Bunk Harmonia," Amy said. "I don't see why you can't be in Bunk Harmonia with Alice, but let me double-check once I'm back in the office."

"Yes!" Maggie cheered as she and Alice high-fived.

"Does that mean you want to go to Camp Athena, Maggie?" Bess asked.

"Definitely," Maggie said excitedly. "This place is cool for a boot camp."

"We don't use that expression, dear," Amy said.

We said good-bye to our "sister species" and to Alice, who had to join her bunkmates. Amy walked us through the campgrounds toward the gate. On the way we passed some girls practicing archery. One girl with curly black hair pulled the bow all the way back before letting it go. The arrow landed with a *thunk* on the round target, just barely missing the bull's-eye.

"Good shot, Trisha!" Amy called. She turned to us and said, "Archery teaches not only skill and precision but safety and responsibility."

Maggie's eyes weren't on the archery practice but on the nearby woods. "Are there bears in the woods?" she asked.

Amy chuckled as she shook her head. "Just some broken-down bunks from an old camp called Green Ridge," she answered. "The camp closed down decades ago. I'm planning to have the buildings torn down by next summer."

"Green Ridge," Bess repeated. "Sounds like the setting in a mystery I just finished reading."

"Do you like mysteries?" Amy asked.

"They don't just read mysteries," Maggie said proudly. "Nancy, Bess, and George *solve* mysteries!"

"Is that so?" Amy asked.

"We're detectives," I said.

"The *River Heights Bugle* almost had an article written about them," Maggie said. "But they were dumped for the Casabian sisters."

"Thanks for the reminder, Mag," George said.

"It's not every day I meet female detectives," Amy said. "How would you like to speak to the girls in a couple of weeks? I like to have special guests visit the camp."

"You want us to be the special guests?" Bess asked, surprised.

"Absolutely," Amy said. "You girls are excellent role models. I'm sure the campers will love hearing you talk about solving mysteries."

"I'll have to ask Mr. Safer for a day off first," I said. "But I'm sure he won't have a problem if I make up the hours."

"Then it's a go," Amy said happily.

"Yes!" Maggie cheered under her breath.

Once we were at the gate, Amy pulled an envelope from her waist pouch and handed it to Bess.

"Here are some papers for your mother or father to fill out, plus a packing list," Amy said. "There are no mobile phones allowed at camp. Oh, and don't forget to pack bug spray, preferably something natural. We have plenty of mosquitoes."

With that Amy reached down to scratch her ankle. She pulled the top of her sock down, and I noticed a tattoo above her ankle. It wasn't a rose or a heart or somebody's name, but a bright yellow sunburst design!

The logo, I thought, my heart racing. *It's the same logo from Roland's Renewal Retreat—and cult!*

4

TATTOO CLUE

I couldn't stop staring at Amy's ankle even after she pulled her sock back up. The sunburst logo was one of the reasons we'd started our investigation of the cult in the first place.

When we were on the beach at Malachite, George had stepped on a hypodermic needle. We found out it contained a mind-altering drug Roland used on his followers. The needle had been discarded along with bottles and jars that had the yellow sunburst logo. And now here was that logo again on the ankle of Amy Paloma!

"Nancy, what's up?" George asked as we walked to Bess's car.

"Huh?" I said, snapping out of my thoughts.

I glanced at Maggie, happily reading the list Amy had given her. The last thing I wanted to do was spoil her excitement, or even worse—scare her.

"George and I were just talking about the camp we went to when we were kids," Bess said. "What was it called . . . ?"

"Camp Tree House!" I said with a smile.

"What did you do there?" Maggie asked. "Did you swim, hike, or play volleyball?"

"Actually, we solved a mystery," I said with a laugh. "We were just eight years old."

On the ride home, we talked about our old days at Camp Tree House. Gradually, I felt better about the sunburst design on Amy's ankle, wondering if I might have overreacted, just a bit. There were sunburst designs practically everywhere—even on the bottle of sunscreen on Bess's dashboard.

Okay. I am not going to obsess about Roland anymore, I decided. *My job at Safer's Cheese Shop starts tomorrow—and not a day too soon.*

It took me, Bess, and George only a few days to settle into a nice, predictable routine—despite

Casabian–mania sweeping through River Heights.

Maggie became a happy camper at Camp Athena. I started my job at Safer's Cheese Shop, where I quickly learned the difference between Swiss cheese and Muenster. The Casabian sisters settled into their new "regular" jobs too. Mia was working as a barista at the new Three Bean Café on Main Street. Mallory was doing her best at the supermarket cash register. But Mandy had already been fired from the preschool, the pet shop, and even the beauty salon (for refusing to sweep "gross" hair off the floor). According to Deirdre's tweets, she had the "perfect" job for Mandy, although she didn't say what it was.

Friday morning I parked my hybrid on Main Street. As I neared Safer's, I saw a crowd in front of the cheese shop. Was Mr. Safer giving out freebies?

I noticed that the crowd was mostly younger girls, many wearing Casabian Sisters T-shirts. Some tees said, I'M A MANDY, I'M A MALLORY, or I'M A MIA.

Forget the freebies. The Casabian sisters were probably inside the store, which explained all the fans.

"Excuse me, excuse me, you guys," I said over and over as I pushed through the crowd. "I work here."

"Nice try!" a girl with long dark hair sneered. "We said that too, but it didn't work."

I glared at the rude kid and the two other girls she was with. Where had I seen them before?

"Nancy!" a voice called.

A police officer who recognized me was holding the door open and waving me inside. I squeezed through the shouting fans, thanked the officer, and burst into the shop at last.

"Made it," I said, sighing with relief.

Looking around, I was surprised to see no Casabians—or customers. Mr. Safer was standing behind the counter, singing and slicing a huge wheel of Gouda while adding his own lyrics to a Broadway show tune.

"Cheddar and feta and ripe gorgonzola," Mr. Safer boomed. "These are a few of my favorite cheese. . . ."

"Hi, Mr. Safer," I said.

"Nancy!" he answered. He wiped his hands on his white smock as he walked from behind the counter. "I tried calling you at home, but your housekeeper told me you had already left."

"Were you calling about what's happening outside?" I asked.

"Well . . . sort of," Mr. Safer said. His eyes darted around the room uncomfortably.

"Is there a special sale?" I asked.

"Heavens, no," Mr. Safer said. He took a deep

breath. "Sorry, Nancy, but I can't have you work here anymore."

I blinked hard. Had I just heard what I thought I just heard?

"I can't work here anymore?" I asked. "Why? Haven't I been doing a good job?"

"Yes, yes," Mr. Safer said.

"I'm friendly to the customers," I went on. "I've gotten great at suggesting the perfect cheeses for recipes and parties—"

"It's not that, Nancy," Mr. Safer said sadly. "I had to give your job to someone else."

"Who?" I asked, still not believing it.

Mr. Safer was about to reply when a familiar voice cried, "Ewwwww! This cheese smells gross!"

I looked past Mr. Safer to see Mandy Casabian coming out of the walk-in fridge. She had a huge wheel of cheese in her arms—and a disgusted look on her face.

"Mandy?" I asked.

"Don't forget to shut the door, Mandy," Mr. Safer told her with a smile. "So far you're doing an excellent job."

But I wasn't smiling. Not one bit. I had a feeling whose idea it had been to replace me with Mandy.

"Do you know how many grams of fat are in one

of these?" Mandy asked as she struggled to place the cheese wheel on a shelf behind the counter. "I'll bet you can get cellulite from just looking at it."

"Mr. Safer," I said, lowering my voice. "This was Deirdre Shannon's idea, wasn't it?"

"Deirdre did suggest Mandy," Mr. Safer said in practically a whisper. "But that wasn't the only reason I hired her."

"Why did you?" I asked.

"Theater, Nancy," Mr. Safer said. "I'm hoping Mandy, Mallory, and Mia will agree to star in my production of *The Three Sisters* by Chekhov."

I stared at Mr. Safer. I knew that when he wasn't selling cheese, he was directing plays at the River Heights Theater. What I *didn't* know was that he could be so star-struck.

"You know theater is my life," Mr. Safer went on. "Besides cheese, of course."

"Okay," I said. "Maybe Mandy and I can both work here."

"I can only afford to pay one worker at a time," Mr. Safer said. "Besides, as soon as Mandy commits to the play, she won't have time to work here anymore—and you can come back."

"Gee, thanks," I mumbled.

"I knew you'd understand, Nancy," Mr. Safer

said. "It's not like you really need this job. After that case you solved on Malachite Beach, you're a famous detective."

Mandy shrieked as the wheel of cheese fell to the floor with a *clunk.*

"It's okay, dear," Mr. Safer said, running to her aid. "Let me give you a hand with that."

I decided to suck it up and not argue, but the whole thing did stink—worse than some of Mr. Safer's cheeses. Deirdre had put Mr. Safer up to this—not just to get her a job in town, but to get me fired.

"Bye, Mr. Safer . . . Mandy," I said.

I was just about to leave when the door flew open. Some guy wearing a wide straw hat pushed past me, bumping my shoulder, not even saying "excuse me."

Mandy can have this job, I told myself as I left the store. *And let Deirdre Shannon deal with the crazy Casabians.*

The crowd went wild when they saw me come out of the store.

"Did you see Mandy?" someone called out.

"Are you going back in?" another shouted. "Can you get me her autograph?"

"No comment," I said, shoving through the crowd. I was happy when I made it through—and even happier to see Bess's car double-parked at the curb. George was in the passenger seat.

"Nancy, what's up?" Bess called.

"You're not going to believe this," I said. "Mr. Safer just sacked me for Mandy Casabian."

George leaned out the window and said, "He gave your job to Mandy? Are you serious?"

"Totally." I sighed. "Deirdre was behind it, but Mr. Safer has his own plans."

Before I could explain about the play, Bess nodded toward the crowd. "Hey, aren't those the girls we saw at Maggie's camp?" she asked. "The ones who were wearing the Casabian Sisters T-shirts in the dining hall?"

I turned toward the store and looked. Bess was right. It was the three rude girls who'd looked familiar to me. So that's where I'd seen them before—Camp Athena!

"That's them," I said. "I wonder if Amy knows they're not at camp."

"I wonder if Amy knows what they're eating!" George said.

One of the girls was digging into a small bag of chips. The two others were stuffing their mouths with candy bars.

"They're not supposed to be eating junk food!" I said. "I thought Camp Athena was all about healthy lifestyles."

"Well, they're not at camp now," Bess said angrily.

"How did they get their sneaky little hands on all that?"

The girl eating the chips noticed us watching and stuck her tongue out.

"Nice," I said.

"Well, this day is off to an awful start," Bess said, leaning her arm on the steering wheel. "You get fired from your job, and some of my dad's tools were stolen this morning."

"What?" I asked. "What happened?"

"Since the paint in his shed is dry, I was hanging the tools back on their hooks," Bess said. "Everything was there, except the hammer and wire cutters. I couldn't find them anywhere."

"Maybe your mom or dad used them," I said.

"I already checked, and they didn't," Bess said. "But we left the window open in the shed last night. Someone must have reached in and grabbed the tools off the table."

"Why'd you leave the window open?" George asked.

"To dry the paint," Bess said. "I'll check again later; maybe they'll turn up."

"That's odd, but maybe your dad forgot he lent them to a neighbor," I said. "Okay, guys, I'd better get to my car and drive home. The less I see of this place the better."

"Wait, Nancy," Bess said. "Why don't we drive down to the river?"

"Why the river?" I asked.

"We saw Ned driving toward the river with the kayak strapped to the roof of his car," George said.

"It's a kayak for two, remember?" Bess said, a gleam in her eye. "Ned's got his car, so he could drive you back to yours afterward."

The thought of kayaking with Ned on the lazy river made me smile. After being sacked, I definitely needed something to smile about—even though I was still kind of annoyed at him for running the Casabian interview instead of ours.

"Well, why not?" I said, opening the back door.

The three of us sang along to Bess's iPod as she drove the car down to the river. The late-summer weather was so perfect, I was happy to have some time off—even if it was because my job had been taken by Mandy.

When we reached the river, I saw Ned's car, parked next to another. I got out of Bess's car and walked toward the water. Ned was paddling his kayak away from shore, but my heart sank when I saw he wasn't alone. Sharing his kayak for two was . . . Mia Casabian!

"Omigod!" Bess said when she saw them.

"Ned!" George shouted, to let him know we were there. "What's up?"

Ned's jaw dropped when he saw me. He forced a half smile before waving with one side of his paddle. Mia waved at us too.

"Sorry, Nancy," Bess said. "Had we known, we would never have brought you here."

"I'm glad you did," I said. "Ned didn't tell me he was going kayaking with Mia."

"Why should he?" a voice behind us asked.

I gritted my teeth. It was Deirdre.

"Hello, Deirdre," I said, turning to look her straight in the eye. "Was this your idea too?"

"Yes, and Ned agreed to do it for show," Deirdre said. "The sisters are working real jobs in a real town. Why shouldn't they date real guys, too?"

"Because Ned is my boyfriend?" I replied angrily. "Of all the real guys in River Heights, you had to introduce her to him?"

Deirdre pulled out her metallic purple smart-phone and said, "Excuse me. I have to make a business call." And then she walked away.

"We can wait here until Ned paddles back, Nancy," George said, glaring at Deirdre. "Then you guys can have it out."

I didn't feel like talking to Ned. Not just because he was kayaking with Mia, but because he hadn't told me. And I had just spoken to him the night before.

"Ned knows where to find me," I said, turning toward Bess's car. "Let's go back to town and grab something to eat."

"Good idea," George said. "I think we all need to cool off after this."

As we approached the car, Bess's phone rang.

"I'll bet it's my dad," she said. "He's probably wondering where the wire cutters and hammer are."

Bess answered, but it was Maggie calling from camp. She was talking so loud and frantically that I could hear her on the other end.

"I'm calling from the camp office phone," Maggie said. "They left me alone for a minute, so I have to talk fast."

"What's up?" Bess asked. "If it's about a care package, forget it. We're not allowed to send junk food."

"Listen, Bess. This is serious," Maggie said.

Bess pulled the phone away from her ear as Maggie shouted. George and I traded puzzled looks.

"Maggie, calm down and tell me what's wrong," Bess said.

I could hear Maggie's voice as she cried, "You've got to get me out of this horrible place, Bess. You've got to get me out *now*!"

5

PANIC AT CAMP ATHENA

"Maggie, you've got to tell me what's going on," Bess pleaded. But Maggie refused to tell until we got to the camp.

"Okay," Bess finally said. "We'll be there as soon as we can."

"Is there a full moon today?" George asked as we slipped into Bess's car. "Too many weird things are happening."

I tried not to think about Ned as Bess drove away from the river. Instead I turned my thoughts to Maggie. Why had she sounded so frantic?

"I thought Maggie liked camp," I said.

"She did," Bess said, shrugging. "She liked being friends with Alice—she even liked the food."

We reached Camp Athena in record time. Maggie was standing at the gate, waiting for us. Once we parked, she ran to us in a panic.

"Okay, Maggie, spill," Bess said. "A week ago you worshipped this place."

"I did, and so did Alice, but it's not the same anymore," Maggie said, talking quickly. "Amy used to be nice, but she's been acting totally weird lately."

"Weird how?" I asked.

"She acts like she couldn't care less about us," Maggie said. "She hasn't posted a schedule for two days. The cooks can't get her to talk about menus or stock up on food, so we've been eating leftovers every day. The tofu is drying up and starting to turn *green*."

"That doesn't sound like something Amy would do," Bess said.

Maggie continued, "She's also been snapping at us—and the counselors. She doesn't even care about the mean girls."

"Mean girls?" I asked.

"Darcy, Lindsay, and Ava," Maggie said, in almost a whisper. "They're from Bunk Diana, and they sneak junk food into the camp, which they refuse to share."

"How do they get their hands on junk food?" I asked.

"Hel-*lo*? They sneak out of camp too," Maggie said. "Either Amy doesn't know or she just doesn't care."

"Okay, so they're sneaky," Bess said. "What makes them mean?"

"Just because they don't share their candy bars?" George asked.

"Are you kidding me?" said Maggie. "They came up with nicknames for everybody. Mine is Magpie. They write nasty things about other campers on the bunk walls, and a couple of nights ago they squirted shaving cream all around our beds and the floor."

Just then I remembered the three girls we'd seen outside of Safer's Cheese Shop—the rude ones with the junk food.

"By any chance, Maggie," I said, "are Darcy, Lindsay, and Ava fans of the Casabian sisters?"

"Totally," Maggie said. "They style their hair like Mandy, Mallory, and Mia and wear the Casabian Sisters T-shirts practically every day."

I turned to Bess and George. "Those were the girls we saw at Safer's today," I said.

"They must have snuck out of camp again," George said.

"You see?" Maggie said. She grabbed Bess's arm. "Can you talk to Mom and get her to take me home?"

"Home?" Bess said.

"Maybe Alice can go home with me," Maggie said eagerly. "Until her mom can take her back to California."

"Whoa, whoa, Maggie," Bess cut in. "Why didn't you call Mom in the first place?"

"Because she never listens to me," Maggie said sulkily. "She listens to you because you're the older sister."

"Fine," Bess said. "But I know what Mom's going to say. She's going to tell you to stay in camp for the next two weeks and tough it out."

"Even with Amy acting so weird?" Maggie asked.

"We can talk to Amy," I said.

"What about the mean girls?" Maggie wailed.

"As long as they're not targeting you, try to be where they're not. There are a lot of different activities at camp, so keep busy. There'll always be mean girls around," George said with a frown. "No matter how old you get."

Like Deirdre Shannon?

But Maggie wasn't buying it.

"*Please*, Bess," Maggie said. "Amy and the mean girls aren't the *only* reason I hate camp, you know."

"There's something else?" Bess asked.

Maggie nodded, her eyes wide. "There's this strange older guy who's been sneaking around camp late at night," she whispered. "He wears a jacket and a big hat that covers most of his face. A couple of nights ago I saw his face, and it was covered with black and red blotches. It looked like his nose was falling off!"

Was this a joke?

"Alice saw him too!" Maggie went on. "Every night when the lights are out you can hear him moaning . . . and screaming . . . and groaning—"

"Okay, Maggie, that's it," Bess said. "Save the scary stories for the campfire."

"You don't believe me?" Maggie asked. She looked desperately at me and George for support.

"Sorry, Mag," George said. "It sounds like you're making stuff up so you can go home."

"You guys!" Maggie groaned.

"Look, Maggie," I said, trying to cheer her up. "Tomorrow's Saturday. Amy asked us to speak to the campers about detective work and solving mysteries, so we'll be here again."

"At least *you* get to go home afterward," Maggie said.

A counselor standing in the distance called Maggie's name.

"I've got to go," Maggie said with a frown. "I'll see you tomorrow . . . if I live that long."

"I thought the Casabians were the drama queens, but Maggie's in training," George quipped as Bess's sister ran to her counselor.

"Maybe," I said. "But, Bess, you really should speak to Amy to make sure all that stuff isn't true."

"All that stuff except the guy with the decrepit nose," Bess said. "I'd be too embarrassed to bring that up."

We walked through the camp, looking for Amy. It did seem as though the campers were somewhat unsupervised. Some were hanging out in front of their bunks. A few counselors were lounging around the pool, sunbathing and texting.

Finally we found her, walking out of the camp office. She bumped smack into us, totally distracted and unaware that we were even there. Almost immediately she flashed a bright smile and said, "Hello, girls. Aren't you a day early?"

"We were visiting Maggie," Bess said. "She told us that camp is kind of different lately."

"Different?" Amy said, her eyes darting left and right. "Different how?"

Bess looked uncomfortable explaining, so I piped up.

"Maggie thinks you might be . . . preoccupied lately," I said carefully.

Still smiling, Amy said, "Is that what Maggie told you?"

"Yes," I said. "She also said—"

"You know, it's normal for girls to get homesick

and miss their families," Amy cut in. "In Maggie's case, it's probably candy bars and ice cream she's missing."

Wow—that wasn't nice!

George looked at Amy and said evenly, "You don't seem to have a problem with the girls in Bunk Diana eating junk food. Or leaving camp to hang out on Main Street this morning."

"Is that what Maggie told you?" Amy said, shaking her head. "She is quite relentless, isn't she?"

"*We* saw Darcy, Lindsay, and Ava on Main Street today," I answered. "Mandy Casabian was at Safer's Cheese Shop, and they wanted to meet her."

Amy turned red. But she continued, "The girls from Bunk Diana had special permission to go to town. They were with a counselor, in case you didn't notice."

"No," I said. "We didn't."

She lowered her eyes, then looked up at the three of us. "I'm been rethinking tomorrow," she said. "And you needn't show up for your little talk."

"What?" Bess said. "You scheduled us more than a week ago!"

"I know," Amy said, smiling slyly. "But I've changed my mind. Mandy, Mallory, and Mia Casabian will speak to the campers."

I stared at her, too stunned to say anything.

"Yes," Amy went on. "Mia will talk about the

importance of school. Mandy and Mallory will share their healthy grooming habits."

"You call wearing tons of makeup healthy grooming?" George asked.

Before Amy could argue, I said, "We can come another day."

And Bess added, "But Maggie's counting on us to be there."

"No, no, don't bother. The more Maggie sees you, the more homesick she'll get. Have a nice day," Amy said, and huffed off.

We stood in front of the office, shocked.

"Maggie was right," Bess said. "It's as if Amy Paloma is an entirely different person."

I hadn't thought about the yellow sunburst tattoo on Amy's ankle—until now.

"You guys," I said slowly. "When we were here last week, I noticed something weird about Amy. She had a tattoo on her ankle."

"Lots of people have tattoos," George said.

"This was a yellow sunburst tattoo," I told her. "Like the logo from Roland's Renewal Retreat and Spa."

"What are you saying?" Bess whispered. "You don't think Amy had anything to do with Roland's cult, do you?" She sat down on the office porch.

"We know nothing about her—other than this

camp. She could have been his follower at one time," I said. "Maybe that's why she's acting so strange. Maybe his brainwashing hasn't worn off yet."

"I don't buy it, Nancy. I can't imagine Amy belonging to Roland's cult," Bess said. "The tat's probably a coincidence."

"I guess," I said—maybe I *was* overthinking it. A person didn't have to belong to a cult to act weird. Just then my phone signaled a new text. It was from Ned. My heart felt heavy as I read the message out loud: "'Nancy, we have to talk.'"

I still wasn't happy about Ned kayaking with Mia, but I decided to give him the benefit of the doubt. Besides, I never passed up dinner at Mamacita's, my favorite Mexican restaurant.

"Honest, Nancy," Ned said while I dipped another nacho chip in mango salsa. "I was just doing Deirdre a favor."

"Kayaking with a famous TV star?" I said. "I'm sure she had to twist your arm for that."

"Deirdre said it was research for the show they were pitching," Ned said. "To see how the sisters got along with average guys. Like me."

I raised an eyebrow as I crunched into my chip. I didn't consider Ned average, and I'm sure Deirdre didn't either.

"Why didn't you tell me you were going?" I asked.

"Deirdre didn't ask me until this morning," Ned said. "I knew you went to Safer's early, so I figured I'd tell you about it later."

"Did you have a good time?" I asked, twirling the straw in my soda.

Ned shrugged and said, "Well . . . It was kind of neat hanging out with a TV star. Mia seemed like she was pretty smart, and really nice, too—"

"Sorry I asked," I cut in. I was about to reach for another chip when Ned grabbed my hand.

"I'm sorry you were hurt, Nancy," he said. "I'm also sorry about the interview in the *Bugle*. Printing a last-minute article about the sisters was my dad's idea to increase readership, not mine."

"So?" I said. "Did the *Bugle* sell out?"

Ned cast his eyes downward as he said, "Kind of, but it's no excuse for not giving you, Bess, and George a heads-up."

I had to finally smile at Ned. He really did feel bad about the article and about Mia. I was about to accept his apology when Deirdre Shannon marched straight up to our table. "Nancy," she said, grabbing one of the chips, "what did you do with Mia?"

"Deirdre!" Ned said. "We're having dinner here."

"What do you mean, what did I do with Mia? Is something wrong?" I asked.

"You bet something's wrong," she said. "Mandy, Mallory, and Mia were supposed to be interviewed on the six o'clock news tonight."

"And?" Ned asked.

"Mia never showed up at the TV station or at her job this afternoon," Deirdre said, pulling up a chair.

That didn't sound like Mia. Of all three sisters, she was the most responsible.

"What do you think happened?" I asked.

Deirdre's eyes burned at me. "You tell me, Nancy," she said. "Because it looks like Mia is MIA."

Missing? The last time Mia Casabian was missing, she had joined Roland's Malachite Beach cult.

"Oh no," I said. "Here we go again!"

WITHOUT A TRACE

"**W**hat do you mean, here we go again?" Deirdre asked.

The last thing I wanted to do was rehash Mia's cult nightmare, especially with Deirdre. I looked at Ned for help.

"Look, Deirdre," he said. "Maybe it wasn't Mia's day to work at the café. She could have forgotten the interview."

"That's a lame excuse," Deirdre huffed.

"I can't imagine Mia forgetting an important appointment either, Ned," I said.

"Well, did you text her?" Ned asked Deirdre. "Or call?"

"Of course I did, but she didn't answer," Deirdre said. "Mia's not even answering her sisters' messages."

"That is weird," I said.

"What did you say to scare her away?" she asked. "You were pretty angry when you caught Ned kayaking with her."

"I was mad at Ned, not Mia. And I never even spoke to her about it," I said firmly.

Deirdre pushed her chair away and got up from the table.

"I'm going to Casa Bonita," she said coolly. "To make sure Mandy and Mallory are safe. Call me immediately if you hear anything about Mia."

Ned and I watched Deirdre storm off. Once she was out of the restaurant, Ned turned to me.

"She's unreal," he said. "What does she think—someone's out to get Mia?"

The thought was a crazy one—until I remembered the carbon monoxide! I started to tell Ned, but then I looked at across the table at his face. We had just made up. No way could I spoil a perfect date with talk about carbon monoxide poisoning.

As we started on dessert, I couldn't stop thinking

about what Deirdre had said. Had something sinister happened to Mia? Were Mandy and Mallory next?

"It is kind of weird that Mia never called or texted," George said. "Out of all three, she's the—"

"Responsible and sensible one." I nodded. "Yeah, I know."

It was Saturday and the morning after my almost-perfect dinner with Ned. Bess, George, and I were headed for the Three Bean Café to talk to Mia's boss. Maybe she'd noticed something strange about Mia or some of her customers. If she had, I wanted to know.

"Maybe the carbon monoxide *wasn't* a careless accident," I said as we walked.

We turned the corner and there was Mr. Safer, busy watering the vividly colored impatiens in front of his shop. Water dripped from the watering can all over his white smock. He smiled and waved us over.

"Ignore him," George whispered. "The guy fired you for no good reason."

"I know, but we have to go into his store," I said. "Maybe Mandy heard from Mia. Then we'll go to Three Bean."

Mr. Safer was humming "Oh, What a Beautiful Morning" as we walked over to him.

"Hi, Mr. Safer," I said.

"Hello, girls," Mr. Safer boomed. He looked straight at me with a big grin. "So, Nancy, when can you start?"

"Start what?" I asked.

"Your old job in the cheese shop," Mr. Safer said. "It's yours if you want it."

I was totally surprised. "What about Mandy?" I asked

"She never came to work this morning," he said.

Another sister not showing up for work? Not good.

"Did you call her?" I asked.

Mr. Safer started watering another planter and said, "She didn't answer my call. Just as well. I don't want her to have anything to do with the cheese shop anymore."

I imagined Mandy dropping more cheese wheels on people's feet or holding her nose every time she had to handle a stinky cheese. But as Mr. Safer went on, I learned that those weren't the reasons he didn't want her working there anymore.

"Yesterday morning I asked Mandy, Mallory, and Mia if they would star in my production of *The Three Sisters*," Mr. Safer said. "All three girls turned me down."

"They're probably too busy," George said.

Mr. Safer's face turned red. "You have no idea how much this play means to me. Having the sisters in it would have brought our theater the publicity it needs—and the advance ticket sales!"

Bess, George, and I had never seen him get so worked up about anything.

"Maybe you can get three other actresses," Bess said. "I'm sure there are some really good—"

"Forget it!" Mr. Safer growled. "It was either the Casabian sisters or no one. I canceled the show."

I was afraid to say another word. He took a deep breath to compose himself, then said, "So, Nancy, when can you come back to work?"

Was he kidding? I should have been excited about getting my job back, but now with Mandy a no-show and Mr. Safer acting so weird, the cheese shop was the last place I wanted to be.

"I'll have to let you know," I said, forcing a smile. "About when I can start, I mean."

"Fair enough," Mr. Safer said. He nodded good-bye, then slipped into the store.

As soon as he left, the three of us started talking as we walked toward the Three Bean Café.

"Do you believe this?" Bess said. "Now Mandy didn't show up for work."

"Did you see how bizarre Mr. Safer was acting?"

I asked as we continued down Main Street. "He didn't seem worried about Mandy, but he was furious that she and her sisters wouldn't star in his play."

"What are you getting at, Nancy?" George asked. "That Mr. Safer was mad enough to harm Mandy, Mallory, and Mia?"

"Maybe," I said.

"Mr. Safer?" Bess said. She shook her head. "Sorry, but I can't picture him doing anything underhanded."

She and George stopped in front of the café, but I had other plans.

"Let's go to Casa Bonita instead," I said. "Maybe Mallory knows something about her sisters that we don't."

Casa Bonita was within walking distance from Main Street. I was relieved to see Mallory when she answered the door.

"I've tried to reach Mandy and Mia," she said nervously as she led us into the house. "They won't answer their texts or calls. And want to know the weirdest part?"

"Yes," I said.

"Their clothes are still in their rooms," Mallory said. "If they left on their own, they would have packed their things."

As we walked into the living room, I was dismayed to see Deirdre, pacing the floor.

"I guess you heard the news about Mandy," she said, looking straight at me.

"We sure did," I said. "And in case you think I had something to do with her disappearance, Deirdre, don't even go there."

"What are you doing here anyway, Deirdre?" George asked. "Why aren't you and Mallory at the police station?"

"If Mandy and Mia are missing persons," Bess said, "Chief McGinnis ought to know—"

"Over my dead body!" Deirdre snapped.

Her sudden reaction was a jolt.

"You don't *want* to go to the police?" I asked.

"Why not?" George demanded.

"I don't want any bad publicity about River Heights," Deirdre said. "The networks would never film the sisters' show here if they thought it was an undesirable location."

"Uh, excuse me," George said angrily. "But without Mandy and Mia, you have no show."

"Mallory, think," I said. "Has anyone been acting strange around you and your sisters lately? Anyone here in River Heights?"

Mallory was sitting on the couch by this time, but nervously twirling her hair.

"So far everyone in River Heights has been really nice," she said with a small smile.

"Could there be a fan who's been acting a little weird?" I asked. "Like being pushy or following you and your sisters around?"

"Just those three Casabian wannabes," Mallory said.

"Wannabes?" I repeated.

Mallory nodded and said, "These three girls, probably about twelve. They style their hair like us and wear Casabian Sisters T-shirts all the time."

Sounded like Darcy, Lindsay, and Ava!

"I saw them too," Deirdre put in, nodding. "They're fans and royal pains."

"Define royal pains," I said.

"My sisters and I called them the junior stalkers," said Mallory. "They would show up at our jobs and follow us home sometimes."

"Did you ever talk to them?" Bess asked.

"At first we'd say hi, but then they wouldn't leave us alone," Mallory said. "One day when they were following us, Mia yelled at them to get a life."

"How did the girls take it?" I asked.

"They were mad—but then again, so was Mia," Mallory said.

George sighed. "Sounds like those brats from Camp Athena."

"Wait a minute," Deirdre said. "Did you say Camp Athena? That's the camp the Casabians are supposed to speak at in about an hour."

"Deirdre, call Amy and tell her it's off," Mallory said. "No way am I speaking without Mia and Mandy."

"Oh, yes, you are," Deirdre said.

"Deirdre!" I said. "Did you forget that Mandy and Mia may be missing?"

Deirdre gave me another one of her bored looks. "Amy doesn't have to know that," she said. "I'll tell her Mandy and Mia had a photo shoot. The kids will still be happy to see Mallory."

I could hear George groan under her breath. I'd always known Deirdre was as cold as ice. I had no idea her heart was too.

"Are you kidding? I'm not speaking at that camp without my sisters," Mallory said. "I'm not going anywhere until I find them."

Then Deirdre snapped. "It's a breach of contract if you don't show up. So unless you're prepared to pay big-time, you're going to camp."

Deirdre's sarcasm and cruel tone wasn't lost on Mallory. Her mouth was a grim line as she glared at her new manager.

"Okay, I'll go," she finally said.

Deirdre was already on the phone with Amy as Mallory walked us to the door.

"Do you think someone around here could be after us?" Mallory asked in a low voice. "Like maybe a crazy fan?"

"I hope not," I said. "But we're going to do everything we can to find out what happened to your sisters."

Mallory waved bye as we walked away from Casa Bonita. I felt bad leaving her alone with Deirdre.

"So what do you think?" Bess asked.

"I think that if a bunch of twelve-year-old girls are the sisters' only stalkers," George said, "we don't have much to worry about."

"Then who *should* we worry about?" Bess asked.

My thoughts turned to Amy. "I know you don't think it's a big deal," I said. "But I keep thinking about Amy's yellow sunburst tattoo."

"As long as you don't think too much," George said. "I've got to run now. I promised my neighbor I'd check out her crashed laptop."

"I've got to pick up those new tools for my dad," Bess said.

And I've got to see what I can find out about Amy Paloma, I thought.

After good-byes, I headed straight home to my room. With Dad playing golf and Hannah running errands, I had the whole house to myself.

I sat at my desk and browsed the web for anything I could dig up on Amy. All I found was current news, like Amy's books and TV appearances, nothing that connected Amy with Roland or his cult. There was a site for Camp Athena, including Amy's mission statement. It was all about empowerment, self-esteem, and the importance of good role models. Ha!

"Some role model Amy's turning out to be," I told myself.

Leaning back in my chair, I gazed out the window and saw someone standing in our driveway, looking straight up at my window. It wasn't Dad, and it definitely wasn't Hannah. It was some guy wearing a white jacket and a fedora-style hat.

A breeze suddenly fluttered the sheer curtain in front of the open window, and when it fell back in place, the man was gone!

I felt a chill, but not from the breeze. It was the strange feeling I got about that guy.

Weird, I thought.

I was about to go back to my computer when my phone rang. Still creeped out by the mysterious figure, I was glad it was Bess.

"I heard from Maggie again, Nance," Bess said, her voice flat.

"Don't tell me she still hates camp," I said.

"She does, but that's not why she called," Bess

said. "She told me that Mallory never showed up to talk to the campers."

Never showed up? The phone shook in my hand as I imagined the sinister possibilities. First Mia, then Mandy—and now Mallory!

"Wait," I said, trying to stay calm. "Maybe Mallory canceled. She didn't want to go in the first place."

"She didn't cancel," said Bess. "Maggie said that when the campers asked about Mallory, Amy just said she had no idea where she was."

"We've got to let Deirdre know," I said.

"I already did," Bess said. "She texted me that she was going to speak to Chief McGinnis."

"Well, it's about time!" I declared.

"Deirdre wants us to meet her at the station too," Bess said. "So we can all talk to the chief."

"Whatever we can do to help," I said. "Tell George to go to your house. I'll pick you guys up in about ten minutes."

I hung up, grabbed my keys, and ran outside to my car. I backed out of our driveway and turned up Bluff Street. From the corner of my eye I saw a red light flash on my dashboard. It was the low brake fluid light.

How did that happen? I wondered.

My car was a hybrid. The generator handled much of the braking, preserving brake fluid.

Making a mental note to get it checked, I kept driving. I made all the traffic lights and turned onto Vernon Street, where the Marvin house stood. I could see Bess and George in the distance. They were hanging out in the driveway, talking to Mr. Marvin.

I stepped on the brakes to slow down. The car kept moving—at full speed. Glancing down at the red light, I saw it still flashing. The brake fluid wasn't just low—it was empty!

Not only couldn't I slow down—I couldn't *stop*!

GRILLED TO OBJECTION

"**H**ELP!" I screamed. I slammed on the brakes over and over, with no luck. The only way I could stop the car now was to crash!

Bracing myself, I gripped the wheel, turning it all the way to the right. With a screech, the car swerved to the side, landing in a deep ditch.

"Nancy!" Bess's voice shouted as my hand shakily turned off the engine. Looking up, I saw her, George, and Mr. Marvin racing down the block toward my car.

"Are you okay, Nancy?" Mr. Marvin asked. He stepped into the ditch, opened the door, and helped me out.

"I'm fine . . . fine," I said. "A little shaky, but okay."

"We saw your car go out of control," George said. "What happened, Nance?"

"The low brake fluid light flashed on," I said. "Next thing I knew I couldn't stop."

Bess and her dad knew a thing or two about fixing cars. While Mr. Marvin checked out my brakes, Bess said, "Even if the light was on, you'd still have enough line pressure left."

"Not if the brakes were *cut*," Mr. Marvin's voice said.

"Did you say *cut*?" I cried.

"I hate to tell you this, Nancy, but someone cut the tubing on your brakes," Mr. Marvin said.

Someone had tampered with my brakes?

"Any idea who it was?" George asked me.

I was about to say I didn't know—until I remembered the strange figure in my driveway.

"There was some strange guy hanging out in our driveway before," I said. "My car was parked outside, so he could have gotten to it."

"What did he look like?" George asked.

"He wore a white jacket and a hat," I said. "If it *was* him, how did he do it?"

"The best way is with . . . wire cutters," Bess said. Then her eyes widened as she waved us away from the car and her dad. "You guys—remember how I told you that my dad's wire cutters were missing from his toolshed?"

"So the guy who stole the wire cutters also cut Nancy's brakes?" George asked.

The thought made my skin creep. "We already think someone is after the sisters," I said. "Why would someone want me?"

"Because you're a detective?" Bess suggested with a shrug. "And he doesn't want you to find the sisters?"

"Right," I said glumly.

We stopped talking as Mr. Marvin came over.

"I can replace the tubing, Nancy," he said. "I can also get Charlie Adams and his emergency truck to pull the car out of the ditch."

"Thanks, Mr. Marvin," I said.

"But if this was an act of vandalism," he said sternly, "it's up to you to go to the police right away."

"We were just about to go to the police," I said. "We'll definitely tell them everything."

"ASAP," Mr. Marvin reiterated, his face grave.

We watched as Bess's father walked back to the house for his tools.

"I guess we'll be taking your car, Bess," I said, gazing sadly at my poor hybrid. I was happy to be

alive, but worried about this stranger in my driveway. Who was he? If he was trying to stop us—
me—from finding the sisters, what would he do
next?

Once in Bess's car, we tried to figure out everything we knew so far.

"So a guy wearing a white jacket was creeping
around outside your house," George told me from
the backseat. "Who wears a jacket when it's eighty-
seven degrees?"

That was a tough question. Everyone we'd seen
in town lately had on sleeveless or short-sleeved
shirts. Everyone except . . .

"Mr. Safer!" I said. "He wears a clean white
smock every day in his cheese shop."

"Do you still think Mr. Safer had something to
do with the sisters going missing?" Bess asked.

"Even if he was upset with Mandy, Mallory, and
Mia," George said, "why would he want to hurt
you?"

"Like we said before—to keep me from finding
out the truth," I said. "Mr. Safer knows I'm a detective too."

We were almost at the police station when Bess
said, "My dad's tools were stolen *before* Mr. Safer
asked the sisters to be in his play. What reason would
he have to do away with them then?"

"Good point," I said, though I was still pretty suspicious of Mr. Safer's weird behavior. And his white jacket.

Bess parked in front of the station. We stepped out of the car, and there was Deirdre Shannon coming out of the building. She looked at us, but kept walking.

"Deirdre, where are you going?" I called. "Aren't we all going to speak to Chief McGinnis?"

"I've said everything I need to say," Deirdre said, brushing past us.

"Okay," George said when Deirdre was out of earshot. "Can someone tell me what that was all about?"

"It's just Deirdre being Deirdre." I sighed. "Come on. We don't need her in order to speak to Chief McGinnis."

The air-conditioned police station felt great as we walked inside. An officer behind the front desk told us to go directly into the chief's office.

"Hello, Chief McGinnis," I said as we filed in.

"I've been expecting you, girls," Chief McGinnis said in his usual gruff voice. "Have a seat."

Three chairs were facing the chief's desk. I sat between Bess and George, eager to talk about the Casabians.

"Deirdre probably told you about Mandy, Mallory,

and Mia, Chief McGinnis," I said. "We suspect foul play. You see, one day when I went to their house, there was carbon—"

"I'd like to ask a few questions first, Nancy," Chief McGinnis cut in.

"Sure," I said, surprised at the interruption.

"Shoot," George said, then quickly added, "I mean—ask away."

The chief looked down at his notes and said, "Is it true you told Ned Nickerson that if you never saw the Casabian sisters again, it would be fine with you?"

Silence.

Why was the chief asking us that?

"You mean . . . when Ned was interviewing us for the *Bugle*," I said slowly.

"I said that to Ned," George said. "I was only kidding."

"How did Deirdre know about that?" I asked.

"Ned told Deirdre, apparently," Chief McGinnis said. "He thought it was funny, but Deirdre did not."

While the chief was focused on his notes, I caught my friends' eyes. What was going on?

"Nancy," Chief McGinnis said, looking up. "You saw your boyfriend Ned kayaking with Mia Casabian a few days ago. How did that make you feel?"

Now I was really confused. Shouldn't the chief be asking questions about the sisters? Or about any suspicious characters we might have seen? But I wasn't about to argue with the chief of police.

"I was upset," I said, still confused. "He's my boyfriend."

Chief McGinnis looked from me to Bess to George.

"Isn't it also true that a certain Camp Athena scheduled you girls to speak, but then you were replaced with the Casabian sisters?" he continued.

"What does that have to do with—" George started to say before Bess spoke up.

"That's right," Bess said. "Amy decided to ask the sisters instead of us."

"How did *that* make you feel?" Chief McGinnis asked. "Angry? Jealous?"

Okay. Now I thought I knew what this was all about.

"Excuse, me, Chief McGinnis," I said. "Are you implying we have something to do with the Casabian sisters' disappearance?"

"I'm only following through on some concerns Ms. Shannon had," Chief McGinnis said, nodding down at his notes.

"Don't tell me we're suspects!" Bess exclaimed.

"I prefer to use the term 'persons of interest' right now," Chief McGinnis said.

"Oh, man." George groaned under her breath.

I was too stunned to speak. I'd always known that Chief McGinnis didn't like me and my friends to take on the same cases he was working on—but to believe Deirdre over us? *Unreal!*

"We had nothing to do with the disappearance of the Casabian sisters," I blurted. "Nevertheless, we refuse to answer any more questions without the presence of my dad—I mean, our lawyer."

"I'm only doing my job, girls," Chief McGinnis said, shutting his writing pad. "That's enough for today."

For today? Did the chief mean there was more questioning to come? The thought made me sick.

"You didn't tell him about your brakes, Nancy," Bess said on our way out of the police station. "Or the strange guy in your driveway."

"Why bother?" I scoffed. "Thanks to Deirdre, Chief McGinnis isn't exactly on our side."

"Oh, but he's just doing his job," George said sarcastically. "Give me a break."

"Well, it's time we did *our* job," I said. "We have to find out what happened to Mandy, Mallory, and Mia—to save them and *ourselves*."

CHILLING ENCOUNTER

"**Y**ou were right not to answer any more questions without a lawyer present," Dad said.

I nodded, not feeling much better. It was only a few hours after our "interrogation." Bess, George, and I sat in my living room while Dad advised us on what to do next.

It was handy having a lawyer for a dad, but I still wished we didn't need one.

"What do you think will happen, Mr. Drew? How serious is this?" Bess asked, wringing the fringe on a sofa pillow nervously.

Dad said calmly, "I don't think Deirdre's word

is enough to get you into trouble, but I will defend you should this go any further."

"Thanks, Dad," I said.

"I can't believe this is happening, Mr. Drew," George said. "We bust crimes, we don't commit them."

"Of course," Dad said. "To be on the safe side, I wouldn't get involved with looking for the Casabian sisters right now."

I stared at my dad. He hardly ever discouraged us from working on any cases.

"Why, Dad?" I asked.

"You don't want to get on Chief McGinnis's bad side, that's why," Dad said as he stood up from his chair. "Especially now."

We kept our mouths shut until Dad left the room.

"What are we going to do?" George asked.

"We're not stopping work on this case," I said.

"You heard what your dad said, Nancy," Bess said. "We can't get on the chief's bad side—especially since we're suspects!"

"You mean 'persons of interest,'" I said with a smirk. "We're already on his bad side, so what have we got to lose?"

"Um . . . our freedom?" George said.

I shook my head and said, "We'll be extra careful

not to cross paths with the chief or any of the police officers."

"Where do we start?" Bess asked.

"I'd like to investigate Safer's Cheese Shop for clues," I said. "I just can't get his white jacket off my mind or how upset he was about his play."

"Yeah, but it's after seven o'clock on a Saturday night," George said. "If the store's closed, how will we get inside?"

I leaned toward Bess and George and whispered. "I still have the keys Mr. Safer gave me when I worked there. He fired me so suddenly, I forgot to give them back."

George cocked her head as she studied me.

"What?" I asked.

"The way you said 'fired,'" George said. "By any chance, are you angry at Mr. Safer because he replaced you with Mandy?"

"Omigosh, George, now you sound like Chief McGinnis!" I said. "I'm not bitter, if that's what you're suggesting."

"Just a thought," she said.

Charlie Adams had returned my car an hour ago. Mr. Marvin had been able to replace the tubing and get the brakes to work like new—although I was relieved when we made it safely to Main Street.

"I didn't tell my dad about the cut brakes," I

admitted as we got out of the car. "He's got enough to worry about."

"What about your dad, Bess?" George asked. "Do you think he made the connection between the missing wire cutters and Nancy's cut brakes?"

"Probably not," Bess said. "He's a great mechanic—but a detective he's not."

I expected the door to Safer's to be locked, and it was. As I fumbled through my pocket for the keys, Bess whispered, "I know this sounds crazy, but I feel like someone is watching us."

"Whoever it is," I said, turning the key in the lock, "I hope it's not Chief McGinnis."

The door swung open.

It was still somewhat light out, so we didn't need to turn on the store's lights and draw attention to ourselves

"What are we looking for?" George asked. "Clues or the Casabians?"

"Both," I said.

Bess pointed to the empty glass case. "Where's all the cheese?"

"Mr. Safer stores it in that fridge at the end of the day," I said, pointing to a large stainless-steel door in the back of the shop. On the wall next to it was the thermostat.

"Does he freeze it?" Bess asked.

"He can if he sets the thermostat low enough," I said. "But it's usually set at refrigerator temps."

"That's a lot bigger than your typical fridge," Bess said. "I'll bet all three of us could fit inside easily."

"What does a walk-in fridge have to do with the missing sisters?" George asked.

Plenty! I thought as it suddenly clicked.

"You guys," I said. "If the fridge could fit three of us, it could fit the three of them."

As we hurried to rear of the store, George pointed to the floor. "Look!" she said.

I glanced down and gulped. Leading straight to the refrigerator door were footprints. *Bloody* footprints!

We walked around the footprints and approached the door. But suddenly Bess said, "Wait!"

"What?" I hissed.

"What if Mandy, Mallory, and Mia are . . . ," Bess started to say. "You know . . . what if they're . . . ?"

"Dead?" George said.

"Don't say it!" I said, not wanting to imagine the worst. I grabbed the handle, gave it a turn, and opened the heavy door.

George took a package of something off the shelf to prop open the door and give us some light.

We walked in slowly, where it was cold *and* pretty dark. Mr. Safer had been meaning to change the lightbulb but never had.

"Anybody in here?" George called.

"Mandy, Mallory?" I called. "Mia?"

I was able to see enough to know there was no one in the fridge but us. I was disappointed not to have found the sisters, but also relieved.

"Wait a minute, you guys," George said, pointing to a shelf in the back of the fridge. "Isn't that raw meat? Mr. Safer doesn't sell meat. What's it doing in here?"

Before we could figure it out—*SLAM!*

I gasped. We were in total darkness. The heavy door had just slammed shut!

George pressed her phone, and it lit up. "I knew this flashlight app would come in handy one of these days," she said.

"The door is locked," Bess said, struggling with the door handle.

"The fridge doesn't lock by itself," I said. "Someone has to do it from outside."

Pressing my ear to the door, I heard something— or someone—running away. I felt myself shiver— not so much from fear, but from cold.

"I hate to tell you this," I said, my teeth starting to chatter. "Not only did someone lock us in, he or she turned down the thermostat."

"You mean this fridge is going to be a freezer?" George said.

Desperate, we tried calling out on our phones but couldn't get signals. We shouted and pounded on the door—until we couldn't feel our freezing, tingling hands.

"No one's going to hear us," Bess said, her teeth clicking from the cold. "I bet whoever locked us in here shut the front door too."

I was just about to wonder what would be worse, suffocating or freezing to death, when the door swung open. In the doorway was the shadow of a tall, hulking man, clutching a giant *cleaver*!

MEAN AT THE BEAN

ess shrieked at the sight of the looming figure. I was too frozen with fear to scream or
to move.

From the corner of my eye I saw George grab a
huge wheel of cheese from the shelf. Lifting it over
her head, she was about to hurl it when—

"Nancy? Bess? George?"

I blinked at the familiar voice. The figure stepped
out of the shadows, and I almost started to cry: It
wasn't a murderer, it was just Hal—the butcher on
Main Street.

"Coming through, Hal!" I said as the three of us

bolted past him out of the walk-in fridge. I almost slipped on a fresh bloody footprint—courtesy of Hal's butcher shop.

"S-s-sorry, Hal," Bess said, her teeth chattering. "But it was a bit ch-ch-chilly in there."

"I'll say!" Hal said as we jumped up and down to get warm. "What on earth were you doing in Mr. Safer's cheese fridge?"

"Someone locked us in," George said. "The rest is a long story."

"Did you hear us calling for help?" I asked.

Hal shook his head. "The fridge in my butcher shop is on the blink," he said. "Mr. Safer told me I could store some of my cuts in his fridge until I got it fixed."

"So that's where all that meat came from," I said, blowing into my hands for warmth.

George pointed to the floor and said, "The bloody footprints, too? Did you make those, Hal?"

Hal's face blushed red. "Afraid so, George," he said. "I accidentally tracked those in while I was carrying in the meat earlier. I felt so lousy about messing up Mr. Safer's impeccably clean floor that I came back to clean them up."

"Does Mr. Safer know?" I asked.

Hal shook his head and said, "Mr. Safer had an important meeting tonight at the theater."

"What about?" I asked.

"Not sure," Hal said with a shrug. "All he told me was that he had to take care of the three sisters."

Take care of the three sisters? Uh-oh. Had Mr. Safer meant the play *The Three Sisters* by Chekhov—or the three Casabian sisters?

"So!" Hal said, raising his cleaver and making us jump back. "You're probably wondering why I brought this with me."

"Uh . . . yeah," George said. "I mean, it's not like you need a meat cleaver to clean a dirty floor."

"Right." Hal chuckled. "I was coming over to clean when I saw the front door half open."

"I must have forgotten to close it," Bess said.

"Well, I was afraid the store was being robbed," Hal said. "So I went back for my biggest, sharpest cleaver just in case I came face-to-face with the intruders."

Hal smiled as he placed the cleaver on the counter. "Instead I came face-to-face with three girl detectives," he said. "So how did you end up in Safer's fridge anyway?"

"Oh," Bess started to say. "We were looking for the Ca—"

"Camembert!" George cut in. "Mr. Safer forgot to pack Camembert cheese for my mom. She needed it for an event she's catering tonight."

Hal looked totally confused. He also must have been wondering how we'd gotten into the store.

George added, "Nancy was also leaving her keys to the store for Mr. Safer."

"Fine," he said. "Now should I call the police about the creep who locked you in the fridge, or what?"

Was he kidding? The last person we wanted to notify was Chief McGinnis!

"We've got it under c-c-control," Bess said, her teeth still chattering. "But th-thanks, Hal."

"Hey, Bess, you'd better put something on to get warm," Hal said. "Here, why don't you take one of these?"

Hal grabbed one of Mr. Safer's white smocks from a hook on the wall. As he held it up, I noticed the big red logo of his store splashed over the front pocket and on the sleeve. How could I have forgotten about the big red logo? *If Mr. Safer was wearing his smock while standing outside my window,* I thought, *I would have seen the big red design, even from up in my room.*

As Hal held the smock for Bess, I noticed something else. The butcher was about the same height as Mr. Safer.

Which gave me an idea . . .

"Hal, can you put on the smock?" I blurted.

Hal studied me like I was from Mars. So did Bess and George.

"I'm not cold, but okay," Hal said as he slipped into the white smock.

I could tell that the smock reached past Hal's knees. The white jacket the guy outside my window wore was much shorter—going just past his waist.

"Thanks, Hal," I said with a smile.

"No problem," the butcher said as he slipped out of the smock. "This has been a strange, strange night."

After showing Hal where Mr. Safer kept the cleaning supplies, we headed out of the cheese shop—but not before I could check Mr. Safer's wall calendar. Sure enough, on today's date he'd written, *Stilton cheese delivery—noon; theater meeting—6:30 p.m.*

"Mr. Safer did plan to go to the theater tonight," I said once we were outside. "Just like Hal said."

"Okay, but why did you ask Hal to model Mr. Safer's smock?" Bess asked.

"Hal's not exactly *GQ* material," George said.

"George, be nice," I said. "The guy I saw outside my window didn't have a red logo on his jacket. His jacket was much shorter than Mr. Safer's smocks too."

"So you don't think the guy in the white jacket was Mr. Safer?" Bess asked.

"Probably not," I said. "He may have been mad at Mandy, Mallory, and Mia, but not mad enough to do away with them."

"Good," George said. "Though we still don't know who cut your brakes."

"Or who locked us in the fridge and left us there to freeze," I said, glaring back at the cheese shop.

We slowly started to warm up as we walked down Main Street. It was packed with people hanging out on a hot Saturday night.

"Let's go warm up with something from Three Bean," I said. "We were going to speak to the owner about Mia, remember?"

We headed to the trendy new café, where people were sitting around tables and in booths. The café was run by a thirtysomething woman named Lola. Lola was originally from Seattle, so she knew a thing or two about coffee.

When we asked Lola about Mia, she replied, "She just didn't show up, which is too bad, because Mia made a mean vanilla latte."

"Did you call her?" I asked.

"I tried several times," Lola said. "She never answered or returned my voice mail."

Lola excused herself to help a barista having trouble with the espresso machine.

We ordered our lattes, then raced to get an empty

booth by the wall for privacy. Privacy was just what we needed to discuss this case—but as we were about to get down to business, we heard loud giggling coming from the next booth.

"Someone's having a good time," George said.

Turning, I saw three girls talking loudly—three girls who by now I knew quite well.

"Guess who?" I whispered.

George looked too and rolled her eyes. "Bunk Diana," she said with a groan under her breath.

"You mean Darcy, Lindsay, and Ava?" Bess asked, surprised. "Does Amy know they're out of camp at eight thirty at night?"

"Would she even care?" George asked.

"Well, I care," Bess said. She started to stand up. "I'm going to tell those girls to get back to camp right now or—"

"Wait—shhh," I hissed. "One of them just mentioned Mia!"

We eavesdropped on Bunk Diana as they blathered on in raised voices.

"Omigod!" Darcy said, laughing. "Can you believe Mia Casabian could be such a witch?"

"Whatever," Ava said. "We got payback, didn't we?"

"Now that they're out of the picture," Lindsay said with a giggle, "we got these!"

Got what?

We turned around to see Lindsay slip on a pair of brown tortoiseshell sunglasses. *Mia's* sunglasses!

"Do I look like a Casabian?" Lindsay asked, posing with the glasses and pouting her lips.

Darcy and Ava screamed with laughter. I was about to say something when Lola marched over to the girls' booth.

"You need to bring it down a notch," Lola told Bunk Diana firmly. "Some other customers have complained about the noise."

"Don't worry—we were just leaving," Ava said smugly. She then picked up her iced coffee and spilled the rest of it all over the table.

"Clean it up now," Lola demanded.

"Us?" Lindsay said with raised brows. "I do believe that's your job."

With that, the girls from Bunk Diana shot out of their booth and the café—giggling all the way.

"They really are mean girls!" Bess said.

We offered to help Lola clean up the mess, but she insisted we relax and finish our coffees.

"Those little creeps have been here before," Lola said.

"Really?" I asked. "Did you ever see them talking to Mia? Or having some kind of fight with her?"

"No fights," Lola said, shaking her head. "But those girls are major pains—as you can see."

I wanted to ask Lola about Mia's sunglasses, but she was way too busy with customers and now the mess Bunk Diana had left behind.

"How did Bunk Diana know all three sisters were out of the picture?" I said quietly over our lattes.

"Nancy, you don't think a bunch of junior stalkers did away with the Casabian sisters, do you?" George asked.

"They may be mean girls," Bess said, "but I'm not sure they're capable of kidnapping . . . or murder."

"How did they get Mia's sunglasses?" I asked. "I'd like to go to Camp Athena and find out."

"I'd like to check up on Maggie, too," Bess said. "How about tomorrow?"

"Can't," George said. "I promised my mom I'd take Scott to a special dentist who's open on Sundays. He cracked a tooth on a popcorn kernel at the movies."

"Ouch," I said. "I can't go tomorrow either. Ned and I are finally going kayaking. Just the two of us."

"Well, it's about time," Bess said with a smile.

My worries and the strong coffee kept me up much of the night. Could twelve-year-old girls really be capable of evil? Did they cut my brakes and not the guy with the white jacket? Maybe he was just looking for an address and not for trouble.

What worried me most was Chief McGinnis. What if Bess, George, and I were arrested for the disappearance of the Casabians? I shook the scary thought out of my head and eventually fell asleep—around three a.m.

As sleep-deprived as I was, the thought of kayaking with Ned made me jump out of bed the next morning. With the help of Hannah, I packed a picnic lunch and waited until Ned picked me up in his car at exactly eleven. He drove us down to the river, where we lugged the kayak from the car to the pebbly bank.

After a quick kayaking lesson, we pulled on helmets and grabbed paddles. Ned slid into the first seat, with me right behind him. I could see how different a kayak was from a canoe. While a canoe had an open seat, a kayak had closed seats called cockpits. In a canoe you either sat on benches or kneeled. In a kayak you sat with your legs stretched out and covered by the cockpit rim.

We each gripped our long paddle in the middle, dipping it into the water from side to side.

"And we're off!" Ned declared as the kayak glided farther into the river.

"Woo-hoo!" I cheered, tempted to splash Ned with the paddle.

Kayaking was just what I needed to relax, but when our arms got tired, we paddled back to shore. Ned and I found a grassy, shady spot to eat and chill out—until my worries came back to haunt me.

Ned listened as I told him all about Chief McGinnis and why we had to find the Casabian sisters more than ever.

"What if we're arrested?" I asked after we finished our sandwiches. The two of us were lying on our backs, staring up at the clouds.

"I promise I'll visit you in the slammer," Ned joked. "I'm sure Hannah will bake you her famous pound cake with a hidden file."

"Ned!" I said. "It's not funny. We're already suspects."

"You mean persons of interest," Ned said.

"Fancy words for 'suspects.'" I sighed.

We held hands and gazed quietly at the sky. Ned thought one cloud looked like his aunt Beatrice's bichon frise, Napoleon.

"The Casabian sisters have a dog back in L.A.," I said. "His name is Peanut, I think."

"There you go thinking about those sisters again," Ned said.

"How can I not?" I said. "Don't you think it's

weird that they just disappeared out of the blue?"

"Of course I do," Ned said. "But I'm sure you, Bess, and George already have a slew of suspects."

"Suspects?" I said, too embarrassed to bring up Bunk Diana. "Nobody solid yet."

Ned suddenly sat up and said, "Enough shoptalk. Let's take the kayak for another spin—before you see a cloud that looks like Chief McGinnis."

"Good idea," I said, giggling.

Ned and I walked hand in hand to the kayak. Once our helmets were on, I slipped into my cockpit. As Ned pushed the kayak into the water I felt something cold and slimy near my foot. Something cold, slimy—and moving!

"Omigod!" I cried, trying to jump up in the kayak. "Something's in here!"

Ned was standing waist-deep in the water as he shouted, "Nancy, don't stand up or you'll—"

"Whooaaa!" I cried as the kayak began to tip. I squeezed my eyes shut as I tumbled out of the boat and into the water.

"Nancy, are you all right?" Ned asked as he helped me out of the water.

"Look inside the cockpit, Ned," I said. "I know I felt something!"

Ned dragged the kayak out of the water and onto

the bank. We peered into the cockpit, and I gasped. Curled inside was a *snake*!

"That's a venomous pit viper," Ned said.

"Venomous—that means poisonous," I gulped. "How do you know what kind it is?"

"I took a herpetology course at the university," Ned said. "I learned about snakes like the one in there."

"What's it called?" I asked.

"I'm pretty sure it's a Florida cottonmouth," Ned said.

Florida cottonmouth?

The name of the snake made my own mouth dry up like cotton. I'd been introduced to a Florida cottonmouth snake not too long ago . . . at Camp Athena!

NO PICNIC

"**N**ed," I said, taking deep breaths to remain calm. "Does the Florida cottonmouth have olive-green scales and a bandit mask?"

"Yeah," Ned said. "What I don't get is how the snake ended up in our kayak. It's not like they're found around here."

"So someone might have put the snake in our kayak while we were cloud gazing?" I asked slowly.

"Who would want to do that?" Ned asked.

Darcy, Lindsay, and Ava, that was who. If they could sneak out of camp to get to Main Street in the middle of the night, they could sneak to the river, too. Though it was hard to imagine them handling a snake, I was pretty sure they'd find a way.

"Ned, there are these three girls at Camp Athena," I said. "They're twelve but going on thirty."

"What about them?" Ned asked.

"All I can say is they're bad news," I said. "Would you mind if I cut our date short? I really have to talk to Bess and George. I'll text Bess to pick me up."

"No problem," Ned said. "I'll stay here and call animal protection. They'll know how to handle the snake."

As I texted Bess, I thought of the madness that had followed us back home from Malachite Beach.

What was happening to River Heights?

It wasn't long before Bess and George pulled up in Bess's car.

"Scott lost a good chunk of his tooth on that kernel," George said. "Who knew popcorn could be so perilous?"

"You think *Scott* had a bad day?" I said. "Wait until you hear what happened to me."

"Oh, no, Nance." Bess sighed. "Don't tell me you had another fight with Ned."

"I found a Florida cottonmouth in our kayak. Sound familiar?" I said.

"Florida cottonmouth," Bess repeated. "That's the type of snake we saw at the Camp Athena zoo."

"Wasn't its name Slithers?" George said.

"Yep. Ned said the Florida cottonmouth is venomous and uncommon in this part of the country."

"Then what was it doing in our river?" George asked.

"I think Darcy, Lindsay, and Ava might have the answer to that question," I said.

"You mean Bunk Diana could have put Slithers in your kayak?" Bess asked.

I nodded and said, "Ned and I could have gotten seriously ill or died had that snake attacked us. Does that tell you they're capable of hurting someone?"

"Like Mandy, Mallory, and Mia?" George said. "I still can't imagine why they'd want to do away with their idols."

"Mia told them to back off, remember?" I said. "Those spoiled brats probably couldn't deal with the rejection, so they decided to get even."

"They did mention something about payback," Bess said. "But why would they want to poison *you* with that snake?"

"By now they probably know we're detectives," I said. "They could have seen us in the café last night and figured we were on their tails."

"So Darcy, Lindsay, and Ava are our new 'persons of interest'?" George asked.

I groaned at the words. It was nice to have forgotten about Chief McGinnis and our quandary for a while—even while I was dodging a venomous snake.

"They're suspects," I said. "And we should be investigating them as soon as possible."

"What about the guy in the white jacket?" George asked. "Shouldn't we be looking for him, too?"

"Yes, but the information we have on Bunk Diana is too important to ignore right now," I said.

"Let's go to Main Street," Bess said. "That's where they're always hanging out."

"Too busy there," George said. "There'll be too many opportunities for them to get away."

She was right. Then I said, "How about going to Camp Athena late tonight? If Darcy, Lindsay, and Ava aren't around, we can at least look for clues."

"What if Amy sees us?" Bess asked.

"Amy Paloma?" I scoffed. "She's so out of it lately, I don't think she'll notice or even care."

"Don't be so sure about that, Nancy," Bess said. "Amy's still the head of that camp, no matter how weird she's been acting."

"Let's take a chance," I said.

"All this for a bunch of twelve-year-olds?" George said.

"A bunch of *dangerous* twelve-year-olds," I pointed

out. "That was a venomous snake in our kayak, and who knows—maybe they locked us in the fridge last night too."

"I'd like to go to Camp Athena tonight," Bess said as she turned her car onto my block. "After everything that's happened, I want to make sure Maggie is okay."

"What about you, George?" I asked. "Ready to go to camp?"

"I'm in," she answered.

"I ran into Mr. Marvin today," Dad said. "He said someone had cut your brakes."

I stared at my father across the dinner table before saying, "He's right, Dad."

"That is serious stuff, Nancy," Dad said. "Why didn't you tell me?"

My shoulders dropped. There was a lot I wasn't telling him about lately: the guy in the white jacket, the walk-in fridge fiasco, and the venomous snake in the kayak.

"I didn't want to worry you," I said. "Sorry, Dad."

Dad heaved a big sigh, like he always did when he was disappointed in me.

"Nancy," Dad said. "Your inquisitiveness probably got you in trouble with Chief McGinnis in the first place."

"No, Dad," I muttered. "It's Deirdre Shannon who got us in trouble."

"Fine," he said. "From now on I want you to tell me these things, okay, Nancy?"

All I wanted to do was change the subject. So I blurted, "Deal," then said, "Could you please pass the string beans with sun-dried tomatoes? They look awesome."

As Dad passed the bowl, he said, "Did you tell Chief McGinnis about your brakes when you were at the station?"

"Not yet," I said.

"Nancy, I want you to tell Chief McGinnis tonight," Dad said. "If you don't want to, I will."

"It's Sunday night, Dad," I said as I spooned string beans onto my plate. "Chief McGinnis is probably having a nice dinner with his family."

Dad didn't argue, so I went on. "I'm going out tonight too. George is picking me up in about an hour."

"Tonight?" Dad asked. He didn't seem thrilled that I was going anywhere—especially after hearing about my brakes. "Where are you going?"

My hand froze over my plate. Uh-oh. I had just promised Dad I'd tell him everything. How could I tell him I was still working on the case? Short answer—I couldn't!

"Um—we might visit Bess's sister at camp," I said, trying to sound cool.

"Camp?" Dad asked with surprise. "In the middle of the night?"

"It's a special program we're part of," I said with a smile. And thought, *Yeah, it's called Catch the Mean Girls.*

"I told you the front gate wouldn't be locked," I whispered when we reached Camp Athena. "Amy is so out of commission!"

Quietly and carefully we filed through the gate into the camp. It was dark, but George lit the way with her trusty flashlight app as we neared the bunks.

"Where's Bunk Diana?" Bess asked.

Before we could look around, I heard a loud creak and saw the back door of a bunk open. Two figures were stepping out, one carrying a flashlight.

"It's Maggie and Alice," I said.

Bess called their names softly. Maggie shone the flashlight straight at us and smiled.

"What are you doing out of your bunk?" Bess asked as Maggie raced over. "And quit shining that thing in my face."

"Sorry," Maggie said, shutting off the flashlight.

"The bunks are pretty cold at night," Alice said.

"We were getting our sweatshirts from the wash line."

"But what are you guys doing here?" Maggie asked, her eyes lighting up. "Did you come to rescue me? Did you come to take me and Alice home?"

"If it's no trouble," Alice said.

"We can't take you home yet," Bess said.

"We're here to work on a case," I said. "So you can't tell anyone, not even your friends, that we're here."

"You have to take me home," Maggie wailed. "I went to the camp zoo today, and Slithers the snake wasn't in her tank. That means she's crawling around here somewhere!"

"Slithers was caught at the river, Maggie," I said. "So you don't have to worry about that."

"Okay," Maggie said, her eyes darting around. "But that guy with the monster face is still creeping around."

"Here we go again," George said with a sigh.

Bess frowned at her sister. "Will you get a grip, Maggie?" she said. "That 'monster man' excuse didn't work for you the first time."

"Um . . . ," Alice said softly. "I've seen the monster man around camp too."

"You?" I said, surprised.

"You want to be mayor of Malachite Beach,"

George said. "Since when do you believe in ghost stories?"

"It's not a dumb story, it's true!" Maggie said, her eyes welling with tears. "Come on, Alice. We're not wasting our time with them."

Alice shrugged before heading to the wash line with Maggie. The two pulled down their sweatshirts, then walked back toward Bunk Harmonia.

"Maggie, Alice, wait," Bess hissed. "Which one of these bunks is Bunk Diana?"

Maggie tossed the flashlight to Bess. "Here," she said angrily. "Find it yourself."

Bess caught the flashlight with both hands as Maggie and Alice stepped back into their bunk.

"Definitely not a happy camper." Bess sighed. "Maybe I should try talking to her again. . . ."

"Will you quit worrying about Maggie?" George cut in. "We should be worrying that Amy could find us and kick us out or even call the police."

"Bess, turn on Maggie's flashlight so we can find Bunk Diana," I said. "It's a lot stronger than George's app."

"Luddite," George called me as she pocketed her phone.

We decided to read the names on the bunks one at a time. The closest bunk was about twenty feet away. We had started up the hill when—

THUNK!

The sudden noise froze us in our tracks.

"What was that?" Bess hissed. She beamed her flashlight at a nearby tree. A chill ran straight up my spine when I saw an arrow lodged in the tree trunk.

S'MORE TROUBLE

"**D**o you see what I see?" Bess gulped.

"Unfortunately," I said, afraid to move.

George was about to yank the arrow out of the tree when we heard giggling in the distance. Turning my head, I saw three girls hurrying in the opposite direction.

"Hey," I whispered. "Isn't that Darcy, Lindsay, and Ava?"

"There's one way to find out," Bess said. She shone the flashlight on the girls. They spun around and stared at us like deer caught in headlights. It was them, all right.

"Wait up!" I called as the girls ran off. "Did you just shoot this arrow at us?"

When they didn't stop, George shouted, "Get them!"

The chase was on. The girls of Bunk Diana picked up speed as Bess, George, and I stampeded after them. Under the moonlight, they charged across the basketball court, where Ava picked up a ball and rolled it in our direction. We sidestepped it and kept running.

We chased them past the pool, but the twelve-year-olds outran us straight to the camp gate.

"Stop, you little creeps!" George shouted.

"Make us, loser!" Lindsay shouted back.

Nobody called George a loser and got away with it. It wasn't long before George caught up with the girls. She grabbed the hood on Lindsay's hoodie and yanked her back.

"Let go!" Lindsay said. She struggled to free herself from George's iron grip as Bess and I rushed over.

Ava and Darcy made it out the gate, but they stopped running when they saw that Lindsay was caught, and trudged back to join their captured friend.

"You're not supposed to be in here!" Lindsay snapped at us after George let her go.

"You're not supposed to be out here," I snapped back. "We saw you trying to sneak out of camp again."

"You're those lame-o detectives, aren't you?" Ava asked.

"How do you know who we are?" George asked.

"That Magpie in Bunk Harmonia is always going on and on about her big sister and her friends," Ava said, rolling her eyes. "Spare me."

"You mean *Maggie*?" Bess said angrily.

"Whatever," Ava said. "We saw you with *Maggie* when Amy was giving you a tour of the camp."

"We also saw you at Three Bean the other night," Lindsay said with a sneer. "We know you're following us."

"We weren't then, but we are now," I said.

"You're also not supposed to be shooting arrows at people," Bess said. "Or didn't you learn that in archery?"

"What are you talking about?" Ava asked.

"We're not even into archery," Lindsay said.

Darcy nodded and said, "It breaks our nails."

I cocked my head as I studied them. They did seem confused and surprised. Could they be telling the truth, at least about the arrow?

"Can we go now?" Lindsay sighed.

"We're not finished," I said. "Before you made a

mess in the café last night, you said something about the Casabian sisters."

"Yeah, so?" Lindsay said.

"So what do you know about them?" George asked.

"We know they're not in River Heights anymore," Darcy said.

"How do you know that?" Bess asked.

"They didn't show up to speak at our camp, that's how," Darcy said. "Which was totally fine with us."

"I'm not surprised you weren't upset," I said. "I understand that Mia called you guys . . . what was it?"

"Stalkers!" Ava said with a frown. "She called us stalkers just because we wanted to say hi once in a while."

"Once in a while?" George snorted. "You mean more like several times a day."

"They should be happy they have fans," Lindsay shot back.

"Who cares about them anyway?" Darcy snorted. "We got even in a big way!"

"Shhhhhh!" Lindsay hissed at Darcy.

"Yeah, Darcy," Ava said. "They don't have to know about Mia's sunglasses—"

Lindsay clapped her hand over Ava's mouth.

"Sorry!" Ava mumbled through Lindsay's hand.

"Look," George said. "We know you have Mia's

sunglasses. What we want to know is, how did you get them?"

The three campers kept their mouths shut.

"You won't be needing fancy shades at juvenile hall," I said. "Which is where you're going if you did anything to those sisters."

"Juvenile hall?" Darcy said. "For stealing a pair of stupid sunglasses?"

"You *stole* Mia's sunglasses?" I asked.

Lindsay groaned under her breath when she realized there was no turning back. "That's how we got even," she said. "After Mia dissed us, we went to the Three Bean Café—"

"You mean you stalked her?" Bess interrupted.

"Whatever!" Lindsay said, rolling her eyes. "We were just going to stick a nasty note on Mia's back or write something on the bathroom wall about her."

"*Nice,*" George said sarcastically.

"Instead we saw her bag behind the counter," Darcy said. "We knew it was Mia's bag, because we saw her get her phone out of it."

"What did you do?" I asked.

"While Mia was busy making a drink," Darcy said, "Lindsay reached over into her bag and grabbed her sunglasses."

"Then we ran out," Lindsay said coolly. "I don't think Mia even saw us in the place."

"We really wanted her phone," Ava said, her eyes shining. "Can you imagine all the celeb numbers she has on that?"

"The glasses are cool enough," Darcy said. "Not only did we get payback, Lindsay got a pair of shades worn by a real live Casabian sister."

"I'll probably get a fortune for them on eBay," Lindsay said. "If I decide to sell them."

"Sell them?" Ava gasped.

"No way, Lindsay!" Darcy said. "At least wait until you go back to school, so you can make everybody jealous!"

"Time out!" George said. "Do you guys have any idea where Mia is now? Or her sisters?"

"Nope," Lindsay said.

Ava nodded her head in agreement.

As irritating as the girls were, I had a hunch they were being truthful about Mia's sunglasses and the missing sisters. But they had yet to answer my other question. The one regarding the snake . . .

"What were you guys doing this afternoon at about one o'clock?" I demanded.

The girls stared at me, obviously not expecting such a loaded question.

"We were at the movies," Lindsay said with a shrug.

"Sneaking out again?" Bess asked.

"What are you, the camp police?" Lindsay said.

"Were you at the movies or at the river?" I asked.

"Why would we go to the fishy-smelly river when we could see *Friends of Summer*?" Darcy asked.

"You mean that blockbuster?" George asked.

"Yeah, and if you don't believe us," Ava said, "Lindsay is wearing the same hoodie she wore to the movies today. It smells like cheese fries, if you want to sniff it."

"Ava, gross!" Lindsay said.

"Yeah, gross!" I agreed—until something clicked. The hoodie had pockets—and pockets at the movies usually contained ticket stubs.

"Show me your ticket stub," I said, pointing to Lindsay's pocket. "The one from the movie today."

"If I still have it!" she said. She reached into her pocket and pulled out a balled-up tissue, a pack of cinnamon gum, some disgusting lint—and a movie theater ticket stub.

"Bingo," I said.

"Wow," Lindsay said, putting it in my outstretched hand. "How did you know I still had this?"

"We're lame detectives, remember?" I said.

Bess and George looked over my shoulder as I examined the ticket stub—which, no surprise, smelled like greasy cheese fries. It was for the movie *Friends of Summer* at twelve thirty p.m.

"All three of you went?" I asked.

"Yeah," Ava said, rolling her eyes. "Would you like us to find our ticket stubs too?"

I handed Lindsay back the stub.

"No," I said. "I have the proof I needed."

When I looked at George, she didn't seem totally convinced.

"You could have gotten the tickets as an alibi," George told the girls. "Instead of going to the movies, you snuck down to the river, where you slipped the snake in Ned and Nancy's kayak."

"Snake?" Ava gasped. "Omigod—what about a snake?"

"Did Slithers escape?" Darcy asked. "If she did, I swear, I'm making my parents take me home. I would never even go near that slimy thing."

I pretty much got that Lindsay, Darcy, and Ava had *not* put the snake in the kayak. I looked at Bess and George, who both gave me a nod. Darcy, Lindsay, and Ava might have been mean—but they were also clean.

"You can go," I said. "Don't even think of going out that gate or we'll tell Amy."

"As if she'd care," Lindsay scoffed.

"Buh-bye!" Darcy said with a fake-friendly wave. "Make sure you watch out for the monster man of Camp Athena!"

"The monster man?" Bess said as the girls walked toward the bunks. "Don't tell me they believe that stupid story too."

When we returned to the tree, we found the arrow still lodged in the trunk. George was reaching to pull it out when—

"Look at the way the arrow is stuck in the tree," Bess said. "Whoever shot at us shot from the woods."

I gulped as I turned toward the dark, foreboding forest. "In that case . . . we'd better get out of here before someone tries again," I said.

"Nancy, look!" Bess said. She pointed to what looked like a piece of paper taped around the shaft of the arrow.

Carefully I pulled the arrow from the tree, then unwrapped what looked like a note.

"What does it say?" George asked.

"'You're getting warmer,'" I read aloud.

"That's the kind of stuff you say when you're playing hide-and-seek," Bess said. "Maybe somebody knows we're *seeking* the sisters."

"While they're *hiding* them somewhere in this camp!" George added.

"The camp grounds are pretty big," I said. "If somebody kidnapped the sisters, they could be keeping them anywhere."

"With so many campers and counselors around?"

George said. "Don't you think someone would eventually hear or see something?"

I cast my eyes back to the woods. Was someone lurking somewhere among the trees? What else was in the woods beside trees and maybe bears?

"Well, the bunks from the old camp are in the woods where the arrow came from," I said.

"So?" George said.

"So an old bunk in the woods could be the ideal place to hide a missing person," I said. "Or *three*."

DARK DISCOVERY

As much as the thought of the dark, desolate woods scared me, I knew we had to search for the Casabians.

"We'll need this in there," Bess said, handing me the flashlight. "My hand will be shaking too much to hold it."

I shone the light between thick trees as we crunched over twigs, acorns, and dead leaves. We stopped when we noticed several paths leading in different directions.

"Great," George said. "Which way do we go now?"

"How about *out*?" Bess said.

As I turned with the flashlight, I spotted an old sign nailed to a tree. The paint was faded with age, but I was able to make out the words CABINS 1–4 and the drawing of a finger pointed toward one of the paths.

"This way," I said.

We walked fifteen feet or so when we reached a clearing. I hardly needed the flashlight, as the moon cast a glow on four bunks with sagging porches and cracked windows.

"Which one do we check out first?" I asked.

"That one," George said, pointing to the last bunk in the row. "There's a light inside that one."

I saw it too—a low, flickering light.

"It could be Mandy, Mallory, and Mia!" Bess said hopefully.

"Or the creep who shot the arrow," George said.

I took a deep breath and said, "We'll never know unless we see for ourselves. Come on."

We headed quietly toward the bunk to a side window, which was cobwebby and cracked. Slowly and carefully we raised our heads to peek inside. There was a candle burning on a small wooden table in the middle of the room.

"I can't see much," George complained. "Too many spiderwebs on the window—inside and out."

"I think I see bunk beds against the wall," Bess said. "The sisters could be lying on them."

I moved closer to the window and saw the bunk beds too. Were Mandy, Mallory, and Mia lying on them? Were they tied up? Or drugged?

"We have to go inside," I said.

"I was afraid you'd say that." Bess sighed.

"We need a lookout," George said. "Bess, since you don't want to go inside, why don't you stay out here on the porch?"

Bess looked out at the dark woods. "On the other hand," she blurted, "it's getting chilly out here. Why don't I go inside with Nancy?"

We walked to the front of the bunk, and George planted herself at the edge of the porch. The door creaked as I opened it. Bess and I walked in, and the first thing we did was check out the bunk beds— empty. No Casabians.

"The sisters may not be in here," Bess said, looking around. "But somebody's made himself at home."

Bess was right. Clothes were draped over chairs and papers were scattered on top of a cubby shelf. A stack of paper cups, a squeezed tube of toothpaste, and a brush stood on the sink in the bathroom. On the floor next to the sink was a plastic gallon jug of water.

"I wonder who's here," I said.

Bess pointed to a bunch of arrows leaning against the wall and joked, "It's either our shooter—or Robin Hood."

We walked throughout the bunk, looking for any clues on the mysterious inhabitant. I came up with an empty blue duffel bag, but it had no ID tag. Underneath the clothing on the chair I found a small plastic bag with first aid supplies—a roll of bandages, a tube of antibacterial ointment, cotton balls, and a plastic bottle of alcohol.

The receipt I found inside the bag told me the supplies had been bought at Hanson's Drugs a few days ago.

"It looks like whoever's staying here was hurt," I said.

"I think I found something too," Bess said.

I walked over to Bess at the cubby shelf. She pulled a folder with faded newspaper clippings from the pile of papers and opened it up.

"It looks like an old article," she said. "Go get the candle so we can see what it says."

I grabbed what was left of the candle and held it over the article.

"It looks like a wedding announcement," I said. "From about ten years ago."

"Who's the happy couple?" Bess asked.

"Good question." I moved the candle over the

faded photograph of the bride and groom, and Bess grabbed my arm.

I stared at the photograph of the beaming couple. Grinning in a dark tuxedo and bow tie was the crazy cult leader and bane of our existence.

"It's Roland!" I said.

And there, gazing lovingly at him in a fluffy white veil, was someone we also recognized.

"Amy Paloma!" Bess gasped.

The caption underneath the photo read, "Marty Malone weds Amy Porter."

"We know Marty Malone was Roland's name before he changed it," I said. "Amy must have changed her name too."

"Nancy," Bess hissed. "Do you know what this means?"

I nodded as I remembered the sunburst tattoo on Amy's ankle. "Amy was more than just one of Roland's followers," I said. "She was his *wife*!"

The door slammed open, and Bess and I jumped.

"George, you scared the daylights out of me," I said. "Is someone coming?"

"No," George said. "But I found something on the porch you ought to see."

"We found something too," Bess said, nodding at the article. "Amy Paloma is—or was—Roland's wife."

"His wife?" George exclaimed. She held up an amber medication bottle. "Wait till you see this. An empty bottle of painkillers."

"Painkillers?" I said, taking the bottle.

"Yeah, now read on the label. Look who the prescribing doctor is," George said, her expression grim.

Bess and I both read the label. The prescribing doctor was Dr. Raymond!

"Dr. Raymond was the plastic surgeon who altered Roland's appearance," Bess said. "So he could hide from the police."

"Now read who the medication is *for*," George said.

I turned the bottle until I found another name. My hand began to shake as I read it out loud: "Marty Malone."

"Roland!" Bess declared, and covered her mouth. "He's alive, and he must be hiding out in this bunk."

"And in River Heights," I said, feeling sick.

"What do you think all those painkillers are for?" George asked.

My eyes darted around while I put the pieces of the puzzle together. Dr. Raymond had performed a lot more than a nip and tuck on Roland—he'd transformed his whole face and hairline—and fast. Maybe too fast.

"Maybe the painkillers are for Roland's plastic surgery gone bad," I said. "No wonder the campers kept seeing a guy with a disfigured face."

"I bet the noises Maggie heard were probably Roland moaning from the pain," Bess said. "She *was* telling the truth about the monster man."

"Amy Paloma has been harboring a fugitive. Someone who could harm the campers," George said furiously.

My heart pounded. The mean girls weren't trying to get us. Neither was Mr. Safer. All this time it was Roland—the demented cult leader from Malachite Beach!

"Do you think Roland followed us back to River Heights?" Bess asked, her voice panicky. "Do you think he wants to get back at us for blowing the whistle on him and his cult?"

"I wouldn't be surprised," I said. "Whatever the reason, we have to tell Chief McGinnis, and we have to do it before Roland comes back and finds us—"

SLAM! The door swung open. Bess shrieked.

We whirled around to see . . . not Roland, but Amy. She shone a flashlight in our faces. "What are you doing here?" she screamed.

"*Us?*" I shouted back. "I should ask you the same question, Mrs. Malone!"

"What? What are you talking about?" Amy asked.

Bess took the wedding announcement over to Amy, who shone the light on it. She let out a deep sigh.

"What a fool—he would keep that," said Amy, shaking her head.

"You were once married to Roland?" I asked. "The guy who ran the cult on Malachite Beach?"

"Who almost killed my friends and dozens of other people," George added.

"Roland and I *were* married," Amy said. "After we separated, I tried to forget him and start a new life."

"Meaning this camp?" Bess asked.

"The camp was part of it," Amy said. "My ultimate goal was to teach healthy lifestyles to young girls. I wanted them to grow up with good self-esteem and stick up for themselves so they wouldn't end up like me."

"What does that mean?" I asked.

Amy took a deep breath and said, "Years ago, before he started his retreat, Roland was arrested for embezzlement."

"Yeah, we know all about that," George said.

"I was part of the crime but managed to escape the law," Amy said. "Roland did his time, changed his name, and began that sick cult you found out about. As successful as he became, he never forgave me for beating the rap."

"After all these years, why didn't you get a divorce? Why are you only separated?" I asked.

"And call attention to myself?" Amy said. She shook her head. "I changed my name too—and my life. I knew Roland would show up someday, but I never expected to see him in River Heights."

"Neither did we," Bess said.

"How long has he been here?" I asked.

"Roland turned up in the camp a little more than a week ago," Amy said, her voice cracking nervously. "At first I thought he came for me."

"Didn't he?" I asked.

"No," Amy said. "He said he came to River Heights to bring down the girls who ruined his life."

"Us," I said.

"You," Amy said with a nod.

"So you went along with him?" George said. "Hiding him in the woods while he stalked and tried to kill us?"

"What else could I do?" Amy asked. "Roland said if I didn't cooperate, he'd turn me in to the police."

As sick as Roland was, I could understand why he was after Bess, George, and me. If it wasn't for us, he'd still be back on Malachite Beach brainwashing his followers and taking their money. But why would he want to hurt Mandy, Mallory, and Mia?

"What did Roland do with the Casabian sisters, Amy?" I asked. "Tell us."

Amy stared at me. "The Casabian sisters?" she repeated. "What does Roland have to do with them?"

"Come on, Amy," Bess said with a smile. "Be a good role model and be *honest*."

"Some role model I turned out to be," Amy said miserably. "I haven't taught my campers anything."

Her eyes darkened when I pulled out my phone. "What are you doing?" she asked.

"Calling the police," I said. "You're protecting a dangerous criminal and putting young girls in danger."

Amy walked toward me, but George held her back. When I tried to call, though, I had no luck. "Darn," I said. "There's no connection in the bunk."

I moved closer to the door to try again, but stopped when I heard someone say, "Going somewhere?"

My blood froze at the familiar, sinister voice. I looked up from my phone to see a hideous face covered with blue blotches and crusted scars.

The palest blue eyes glared at me from under a straw hat, the unmistakable eyes of *Roland*.

13

ROLAND'S REVENGE

Roland towered over me as he backed me up into the bunk. He wore the sickeningly familiar white jacket and a sinister grin on his ruined face.

"I wouldn't bother calling Chief McGinnis," Roland snarled. "He doesn't have a very good record of believing you and your friends."

"He'll believe us now," George said angrily. She caught Bess's and my eyes. "No way is this jerk holding us hostage. Come on."

George was the first to charge toward the door. Gathering our guts, Bess and I followed. We made it halfway when Roland reached down to pick up an arrow.

"Guard the door, Amy," he ordered as he brandished the arrow at us. "Now!"

Amy flitted to the door like an obedient puppy. It was plain to see how scared she was of her husband—and staring at the arrow in Roland's hand, so was I.

"How did you know about Chief McGinnis?" I asked, trying to keep my voice steady.

"I know more about you than you think," Roland said with a grin. "For instance, I know you don't really like snakes, you prefer warm weather to freezing-cold freezers, and you're an excellent driver until your brakes go out."

"Since you seem to know so much, Roland," I said, emphasizing his name, "where are Mandy, Mallory, and Mia?"

Roland waved his free hand with a snort.

"Those ridiculous sisters." He sighed. "They were just a nuisance, something to get rid of so I could focus on my main objective. You."

"Get rid of?" I said. "As in poisoning them in their house with carbon monoxide?"

Roland shrugged and said, "Can't blame a guy for trying."

Roland's words made me queasy. Had he succeeded in getting rid of the Casabians?

"What did you do with them?" George demanded, talking a step toward Roland.

"Get back!" he shouted. "If it weren't for you, I'd still have my beloved retreat on Malachite Beach, I wouldn't be looking like a monster, and I wouldn't be in such pain."

Roland threw back his head and moaned. As he lowered the arrow, George reached for it—until Roland quickly raised his arm.

"Now I've got River Height's star girl detectives exactly where I want them," he said with a maniacal grin. "Revenge will be so sweet."

I held my breath. Roland was holding the pointed arrowhead directly under my eye.

"As a very wise man once said," Roland went on, chuckling, "garbage in . . . garbage out."

I was so weak with fear that my knees began to buckle, and I started to black out.

"Drop that!" Amy shouted.

I looked up to see Amy standing behind Roland, a chair in her raised hands.

"I said drop it!" Amy shook the chair. "Or I'll smash this on your head!"

Roland stared at Amy but did as she ordered. He didn't notice George reaching out to pick up the arrow.

"In case you haven't checked, you're still my wife, Amy," Roland said. "So don't do anything stupid!"

"The only stupid thing I did was marry you!" Amy shouted. "You may have had me under your thumb then—but not anymore."

She looked past a stunned Roland at me. "Go outside and call the police, Nancy," she said. "Now."

I nodded and ran to the door. As I pulled it open, I heard an amplified voice crackle through a bullhorn: "Amy Paloma, Marty Malone—come out with your hands over your head."

I shaded my eyes, blinded by the beam of a powerful flashlight. Three figures stood before the porch: two police officers and Chief McGinnis.

"Come on out, Nancy," Chief McGinnis said. "Are Bess and George okay?"

"We're fine," George said as she and Bess joined me on the porch.

The officers charged inside the bunk, where I could hear Roland arguing. My heart was still racing, although I knew we were finally safe.

"Thanks, Chief McGinnis," I said. He helped us down from the creaky porch.

"Don't thank me," Chief McGinnis said with a grin. "Thank Maggie Marvin and Alice Bothwell."

"What do you mean?" Bess asked, surprised.

"Turns out Maggie and Alice had seen the camp monster going into the woods and were worried about you," the chief explained. "They woke some counselors and convinced them to call the station," he explained.

"Good for Maggie and Alice!" Amy's voice said.

We turned to see Amy and Roland being led out of the bunk, their hands cuffed.

Roland was struggling against his cuffs. "Officers, I've done nothing wrong. Amy is the fugitive. She's the real criminal."

"Save it for the station, Marty," Chief McGinnis said, spitting out Roland's real name. "We know all about you and your wife. What we didn't know until now was that you were in River Heights."

The three of us watched as the officers led Roland and Amy out of the woods.

"I guess I owe you girls an apology," Chief McGinnis told us, "For accusing you of the Casabian sisters' disappearance."

The Casabian sisters!

Roland had never told us what he did to them!

"Chief McGinnis, Roland—or Marty Malone—wanted to get rid of the sisters to get to us," I said. "He already tried poisoning them with carbon monoxide."

Chief McGinnis shook his head with a smile. "I spoke to them," he said. "Mandy, Mallory, and Mia are just fine."

"What? Where are they?" Bess asked.

"How did you find them?" George asked.

"I'll fill you in on everything after we book Mr. and Mrs. Malone," Chief McGinnis said. "In the meantime, why don't you help the campers and counselors call home? Like Green Ridge, Camp Athena will soon be history."

Bess, George, and I were too relieved and exhausted to speak as we followed Chief McGinnis out of the woods. I was happy Roland would finally get what he deserved. Secretly I hoped Amy would get some kind of break for trying to start a new life and for saving ours. *That* I would leave to the police and the legal justice system.

Back on the campgrounds, the girls and their counselors were buzzing about the excitement. I caught the eye of Lindsay standing in the crowd with Darcy and Ava. Instead of scowling at us like she usually did, she smiled and gave us a big thumbs-up.

"Are we some kind of heroes?" George asked.

"Here come the real heroes," I said as Maggie and Alice raced over.

"Good job!" Bess said, hugging and high-fiving her sister. "I believe we have another detective team in River Heights!"

"Alice Bothwell, Private Investigator," Alice said thoughtfully. "I guess I could be mayor of Malachite Beach *and* a detective someday."

"With a little multitasking," I added.

"Now do you believe us about the monster of Camp Athena?" Maggie asked.

"He was a monster, all right," I said with a shudder.

"And guess what, you guys?" George told the girls. "You're finally going home."

"Home?" Maggie said.

"Too bad," Alice said with a grin. "We were just starting to have fun!"

"So what did happen to the Casabian sisters?" Ned asked, pushing his recorder closer to Bess, George, and me.

It was only two days after Roland's capture. My two friends and I sat in Sylvio's, being interviewed for the second time by Ned.

"Before I answer that question," I teased, "do you promise our interview will appear in the *Bugle* this time?"

"Page four!" Ned said with a nod.

"And you promise not to replace it at the last minute with any Hollywood gossip?" Bess asked.

"I promise, I promise!" Ned laughed.

"In that case, Nancy," George said, "spill."

"Okay, here goes," I said. "The Casabian sisters left River Heights one at time and for different reasons. That's what they said when we spoke to them on the phone the other day."

"What kind of reasons?" Ned asked.

"Well," I said sprinkling oregano on my slice, "Mia totally hated the idea of another reality show. Mandy hated working real jobs like the one she got at Safer's Cheese Shop."

"And Mallory?" Ned asked.

"That's easy," George blurted. "She hated Deirdre Shannon."

"Don't quote her on that," I said quickly.

"How's this for a happy ending?" Bess said, twirling the straw in her lemonade. "Now all three sisters are home where they belong."

"That must be Malachite Beach," Ned said.

"Nope," I said. "Alice went home to Malachite Beach. Mandy, Mallory, and Mia are in Ohio."

"Ohio?" Ned asked.

"Where their parents and brother still live," I said. "I guess they finally realized their true reality."

"Wow," Ned said. "Didn't they tell one another where they were going? I mean, from what I heard, they didn't even pack their bags."

"It was part of their plan," I said.

"As in secret plan?" Ned asked, his eyebrows flying up. "This is getting good!"

I nodded. "They didn't want anyone here—

especially Deirdre—to try to stop them," I said. "So they each disappeared without a trace. Mallory knew all along, but she 'played' us, just like the 'reality' actress she is."

"They said they had meant to call us from Ohio," George said. "Unfortunately, they didn't call fast enough."

That was for sure. I shivered, remembering being framed for the disappearance of the sisters and coming within inches of death at the hands of Roland.

"Are you guys worried?" Ned asked.

"Worried about what?" I asked.

"About Roland escaping again," Ned said.

I looked at Bess and George before all three of us shook our heads.

"No," I told Ned. "Roland—or Marty Malone—has never dealt with River Heights justice before."

"Can you elaborate on that?" Ned asked.

"Sure," I said. "River Heights may be considered rinky-dink to someone from Malachite, but we have the best police, the best lawyers—"

"And the best girl detectives," George said. She grinned as she picked up another slice. "And you can quote me on *that*."

CAROLYN KEENE
NANCY DREW

GIRL DETECTIVE

Secret Sabotage

Serial Sabotage

Sabotage Surrender

Secret Identity

Identity Theft

Identity Revealed

Model Crime

Model Menace

Model Suspect

INVESTIGATE THESE THREE THRILLING MYSTERY TRILOGIES!

FRANKLIN W. DIXON

THE HARDY BOYS

Undercover Brothers®

INVESTIGATE THESE TWO ADVENTUROUS MYSTERY TRILOGIES WITH AGENTS FRANK AND JOE HARDY!

#28 Galaxy X

#29 X-plosion!

#30 The X-Factor

#31 Killer Mission

#32 Private Killer

#33 Killer Connections

From Aladdin
Published by Simon & Schuster

IF YOU ♥ THIS BOOK,
you'll love all the rest from

YOUR HOME AWAY FROM HOME:

AladdinMix.com

HERE YOU'LL GET:

- ♥ The first look at new releases
- ♥ Chapter excerpts from all the Aladdin M!X books
- ♥ Videos of your fave authors being interviewed